THE LITTLE VAMPIRE TAKES A TRIP

THE LITTLE VAMPIRE

TAKES A TRIP

Previously titled
The Vampire Takes a Trip

BY **Angela Sommer-Bodenburg**

NEWLY TRANSLATED BY **Ivanka Hahnenberger and Elowyn Castle**

ALADDIN

New York   London   Toronto   Sydney   New Delhi

ALADDIN

An imprint of Simon & Schuster Children's Publishing Division

1230 Avenue of the Americas, New York, New York 10020

First Aladdin hardcover edition November 2023

Text copyright © 1980 by Angela Sommer-Bodenburg

English language translation copyright © 2023 by Simon & Schuster, Inc.

Originally published in Germany by Rowohlt Taschenbuch Verlag GmbH as *Der kleine Vampir verreist*

Previously titled *The Vampire Takes a Trip*

Jacket illustration copyright © 2023 by Daniel Duncan

Also available in an Aladdin paperback edition.

All rights reserved, including the right of reproduction in whole or in part in any form.

ALADDIN and related logo are registered trademarks of Simon & Schuster, Inc.

For information about special discounts for bulk purchases, please contact Simon & Schuster Special Sales at 1-866-506-1949

or business@simonandschuster.com.

The Simon & Schuster Speakers Bureau can bring authors to your live event. For more information or to book an event contact the Simon & Schuster Speakers Bureau at 1-866-248-3049 or visit our website

at www.simonspeakers.com.

Series designed by Laura Lyn DiSiena

Interior designed by Irene Vandervoort

The text of this book was set in ITC Clearface Pro.

Manufactured in the United States of America 1023 BVG

10 9 8 7 6 5 4 3 2 1

Library of Congress Control Number 2023945680

ISBN 9781534494145 (hc)

ISBN 9781534494138 (pbk)

ISBN 9781534494152 (ebook)

This book is for all
who would like to become Rudolph's travel companion,
and for Burghardt,
who has been mine since time immemorial.

Checking the Map

It was a mild spring evening. The sweet smell of jasmine filled the air, while moonlight bathed the neighborhood in a soft silver light.

As the big hand moved to twelve, the clock began to strike: one, two . . .

The little vampire sat at the top of a chestnut tree and quietly counted along: ". . . seven, eight, nine." Nine o'clock—surely that wasn't too early to visit his friend Tony? His parents must have left to go to the movies or to see friends, as they did almost every Saturday night.

This was always really great, thought the little vampire, because it meant that Tony had been able to accompany him on many of his nocturnal adventures. For example, the vampire ball, where Tony had dressed up as a vampire and danced with him so that the other vampires wouldn't suspect that Tony was human. Tony had looked really funny when he was forced to look lovingly at the vampire as they danced.

The little vampire giggled. He was starting to get hot in his woolen tights and the two capes he was wearing, one of which was for Tony. He decided to fly to Tony's window and knock.

The curtains in Tony's room were closed, but the little vampire was able to peep into the room through a gap in the curtains. He saw Tony sitting on the floor, looking over a large map lit by the light of the desk lamp.

The vampire tapped on the window with his long fingernails, and, cupping his hands around his mouth, called out, "It's me, Rudolph!"

Tony lifted his head. He looked startled at first, but then his expression brightened. He went to the window and opened it.

"Hello," he said. "For a second there I thought you were Aunt Dorothee."

The vampire laughed. "You don't have to worry about Aunt Dorothee tonight. She's flown off to a dance in the village," he said as he climbed into the room.

"To dance?"

"Of course not. She's probably lurking in front of the dance hall, waiting for the first guests to head home. And then . . ." He let out a cackling laugh, and Tony saw his pointy, needle-sharp fangs. As usual, they gave him goose bumps. "She actually can't stand the people in the village," the vampire continued cheerfully. "Last time, they all had so much to drink that Aunt Dorothee lay in her coffin for two nights before she felt well enough to go out again."

"Yuuuck," said Tony quietly. He preferred not to be reminded that vampires—including his best friend—survived on blood. Fortunately, Rudolph made sure he always ate before he came to visit.

The little vampire pointed to the map. "Homework?"

"No," said Tony darkly. "I went to visit a farm with my parents this afternoon. Here, in the middle of nowhere."

He pointed to a dot on the map, and the vampire leaned

forward to read the place-name: "Little Ol' Molting."

"Yup, that's the name of the Podunk town," said Tony. "My parents want to spend a week on a farm there."

"Alone?"

"No, I have to go with them, of course. Dad says they'll be able to really relax there, far away from the noise of the big city, breathing fresh country air, going for walks. . . ." At these last words, Tony sounded so disgusted that the little vampire had to laugh.

"It can't be that bad," he said.

"How would you know?" exclaimed Tony, his face turning red with anger. "Only cows, clucking chickens, and neighing horses as far as the eye can see. And absolutely nothing to do!"

"What about riding?"

"Pah, riding! On those old swayback things!"

"How about on a tractor?"

"Bo-ring! I want to go on vacation somewhere where you can really have fun. But in Little Ol' Molting—" Upset, he ran his finger over the map. "Just listen to the names of the towns around it: Big Ol' Molting, Deadmoulton, Old Cairn, New Cairn. What on earth could possibly be exciting about those nowhere towns?"

Tears welled up in Tony's eyes, and he quickly wiped them away so that the little vampire wouldn't notice. His parents had planned a week's vacation and hadn't even asked his opinion! They'd decided on a farm in the middle of nowhere and expected him to be happy about it!

Now, *he* would have known where to go! A real resort, for example, with a swimming pool, lots of restaurants, movie theaters, clubs. But they hadn't even considered what *he* might've wanted!

"It sounds pretty nice to me," said the vampire.

"Not to me!" said Tony, frustrated. Then he paused. He had an idea. "You really think so?" he asked.

"Well, the place-names sound promising—as if there could be vampires there. You might get to know a few, if you walk through Little Ol' Molting cemetery after dark," said the little vampire.

"Me?" said Tony cryptically, and with a grin, he added, "We!"

The vampire looked confused.

"Whadda you mean, 'we'?"

"I mean," said Tony, "you're coming with me. If we go together, it'll be the most exciting vacation ever!"

"But—" The vampire was speechless.

"Didn't you just say it sounded pretty nice?" Tony reminded him.

"I meant for you."

"What's good for me is good for you. Or are we not friends?"

"But—"

"And didn't I help you when you were banished from the crypt and left homeless with your coffin? Didn't I hide you in the basement?"

"But—"

"Well, now you can do something for me!"

The vampire turned away and began to chew his nails. "It's all too sudden for me," he murmured miserably.

"We vampires don't make hasty decisions!"

"Who said anything about hasty?" exclaimed Tony. "We're not leaving until next Sunday. We have plenty of time to figure everything out. Like how we're going to send your coffin to Little Ol' Molting, for example."

The vampire winced. "But what if it gets lost on the way?" he whined. "That would be the end of me!"

"Exactly. That's why we have to plan everything carefully. Maybe we could—"

At that moment, they heard voices at the front door.

"My parents!" exclaimed Tony, frightened. "They never come back this early."

In one jump the vampire was on the windowsill with his cape spread out.

"Come back tomorrow night!" Tony called after him. "We'll work out the rest of the details."

Easily Frightened

Tony closed the window, drew the curtains, and started folding up the map. His mother would knock the minute she saw the light on under the door.

"Tony, are you still awake?" she asked through the door, and knocked.

"Hmm," he mumbled.

She came in and looked at him in surprise. "You haven't even put your pajamas on yet?"

"No."

"And it's stuffy in here again. . . ."

With a few quick steps, she went to the window and opened it wide.

"You should always let in some fresh air before going to bed, Tony. A stuffy room is unhealthy!"

"Yes, Mom," Tony said, giggling to himself. She couldn't know that it was Rudolph's special odor that she was smelling.

"How come you're back so early?" he asked.

"Why, were you planning something?"

"No. I just wanted . . ."

". . . to watch TV, I bet?"

"Me? Television? No, I've been looking at the map!" Since he couldn't fold it properly anyway, he spread it out on the floor again. "I wanted to see what there was around Little Ol' Molting."

"And what did you find?"

"Deadmoulton—it sounds really interesting. Maybe there are some vampires there."

"Vampires, vampires!" His mother suddenly sounded annoyed. "All you can think about is vampires. It's probably because of all those vampire stories you're always reading!"

She went to the bookshelf and took out some of Tony's favorite books.

"*Dracula, Dracula's Revenge, The Twelve Scariest*

Vampire Stories Ever, In the House of Count Dracula, Laughter from the Crypt." One by one, she dropped the books on the bed. "Just reading out the titles gives me the creeps."

Every time a book landed on the bed, Tony winced. However, he didn't say anything. He didn't want to upset his mother any more than she already was. Otherwise, she might take the books away from him.

"You're easily frightened," he said as he carefully picked up the books and put them back on the shelf.

"So are you. If you could only hear yourself scream in your sleep!"

"That just means I'm dreaming about school."

"Oh, really? Is there a Dorothee in your class?"

"Dorothee?" Tony paled.

"Last night you shouted, 'Aunt Dorothee, please, don't bite me!'"

"Well, uh"—he searched carefully for the right words—"that's the temporary cleaning lady at school. She has really pointy teeth. And the other day, I forgot my gym bag in class and went back to get it, and she was there . . . and she looked at me with her sharp, pointy teeth. . . .”

He had broken out into a sweat telling his story. His mother just smiled, clearly not convinced.

“Knowing you, you wouldn't walk an inch for a forgotten gym bag.”

“There was money in it,” he said quickly.

How was it that his mother caught him every time? He could come up with the best stories, but she saw through them anyway. Only one thing ever worked: telling the truth.

“All right.” He took a deep breath. “Aunt Dorothee is Rudolph the little vampire's, Anna the Toothless's, and Gregory the Gruesome's aunt. She's the most dangerous of the Sackville-Bagg vampires.”

For a moment, his mother was too stunned to say anything. Then her eyes narrowed and she exploded, “I've had enough of these vampire stories!”

“Dad hasn't,” said Tony.

“What?”

Tony nodded toward the door.

"He just turned on the TV, and there's a vampire movie on. *Dracula, the Lonely Wanderer*."

The sound of the television came softly into the room.

"You seem to be in the know," said his mother. Tony felt himself go red. Of course, he couldn't admit that he had been looking forward to the movie all evening. "Then it's true."

"What?"

"That you wanted to watch TV. And if we hadn't come home early—"

"But, Mom!" said Tony indignantly.

"Yeah, yeah," said his mother. "But this time you're not going to get away with it. You're going to change into your pajamas and go to bed."

"All right," Tony muttered, trying to look very disappointed. He had to bite his lip so as not to laugh. His mother had obviously forgotten that he had his own TV in his room!

Bad Books

At breakfast the next morning, Tony's father asked, "So, you've decided you do want to go to the farm, after all?"

"Hmm," Tony responded evasively.

"But I couldn't really understand why you wouldn't want to, anyway," his father reflected. He poured himself another cup of coffee and added, "It's every city kid's dream: climbing trees, building tree houses, night wildlife walks, scavenger hunts."

Tony looked up from his plate in surprise. "Is that the kind of stuff we're gonna do? I thought you just wanted to go for plain old walks."

His parents exchanged looks.

"We do, yes," said his father. "We're going there to

relax, and scavenger hunts are probably a bit too strenuous for us." When he saw Tony's disappointed face, he quickly added, "But on the farm there's plenty for you to do without us. You can help feed the animals, ride in the fields with the farmer. And you can play with the farm kids. Isn't the boy the same age as you?"

"Tony's a year younger," corrected his mother.

"Oh, him," said Tony, dismissing him with a wave of his hand. "He's only interested in knights. He told me he has five hundred toy knights in his room."

His father laughed. "Then you're a good match. He has his knights, and you have your vampires."

Tony gasped. It was ridiculous to equate knights with vampires!

"Knights died out centuries ago!" he exclaimed. "Chivalry is from the Middle Ages."

"But vampires still exist?" his mother asked dryly.

Tony quickly bent over his plate to hide his grin.

"Of course not," he said, holding back his laughter

with difficulty. "Vampires only exist in books—bad ones," he added. "Right?"

How does a vampire go on vacation? Tony spent all day Sunday thinking about this, but instead of coming up with ideas, he came up with a list of issues. The crux of the problem being that vampires have to sleep in their own coffins. So they can only go on vacation if they take their coffins with them. But how? You can't put them in a suitcase. And they're too heavy for a vampire to carry one under his arm while flying.

But if Rudolph took the train, could they send it as luggage in the baggage car? Tony wondered. He'd read somewhere that when people died while traveling, they were sent back home in coffins. But wouldn't the railway officials become suspicious if he, Tony, wanted to check in a coffin as luggage?

He sighed. If only he had someone he could discuss this with! But he couldn't say anything to his parents, and the little vampire didn't like to be bothered with problems.

Tony's eyes went to his books. Wasn't there a story in one of them about a vampire going on a trip? Maybe he could get tips from there. Of course: Bram Stoker's *Dracula*! Count Dracula traveled by ship from his castle in Transylvania to England!

Excited, Tony took the book off the shelf. It had been a few months since he had last read it, so he couldn't remember all the details. But he still knew that fifty large boxes played an important role in the count's travel arrangements. The book began with the diary entries of Jonathan Harker, a lawyer from England, whom Dracula had lured to his castle.

"'30 June, morning,'" Tony read. "'The great box was in the same place, close against the wall, but the lid was laid on it, not fastened down, but with the nails ready in their places to be hammered home. . . . I raised the lid, and laid it back against the wall. . . . There lay the Count, but looking as if his youth had been half renewed . . . the mouth was redder than ever, for on the lips were gouts of fresh blood. . . . As I write there is in the passage below a sound of many tramping feet and the crash of weights being set down heavily, doubtless the boxes, with their freight of earth. There is a sound of hammering; it is the box being nailed down.'"

The box—that was Dracula's coffin. But why did he need the other boxes? So he couldn't be found so easily? With only one box, someone could easily open it, but with fifty . . . Not a bad idea, Tony thought admiringly. Unfortunately, this strategy was out of the question for him and Rudolph, because they didn't have the means to transport the boxes, nor were they going by ship.

It was starting to get dark out. Tony's father came in with a sandwich and a glass of milk. "Your mother says it's time for you to go to bed," he said, putting the glass next to Tony on the bedside table. Curious, he leaned forward and tried to read the title of the book.

"Vampire stories?" he asked.

"I'm trying to solve a problem," Tony explained, and closed the book. He put it on his pillow facedown and took half a cheese sandwich. "Maybe you can help me," he said.

"Me?"

"You work for a shipping company."

"Yes . . ."

"So, you send things around a lot."

His father laughed. "Yes."

"I have a friend," said Tony, "who wants to send something."

"Yeah? What?"

"A box. About that long." Tony spread out his arms. "Maybe even a little longer."

"Pretty big, isn't it?" said his father. He didn't seem to be taking Tony's question very seriously.

"What's your friend sending in his box? Pearls? Gold? Gemstones?"

Tony gritted his teeth angrily. "I thought you wanted to help me."

"I do! But I need to know what he's sending." And with a glance at Tony's book, he added, "It could be a vampire coffin, right? We don't ship things like that. We're a respectable company."

At first Tony was afraid that his father might be suspicious, but then he realized that he was only making fun of him. So Tony didn't mince his words.

"What a shame!" he said bitterly. "It actually *is* a vampire coffin."

Of course, his father didn't believe a word he said.

"In that case," he quipped, "your friend should try a funeral home." And he headed for the door.

"Mom and I are going for a walk," he said.

"Will you be out long?" asked Tony, surprised.

"Long enough for you to be asleep by the time we get back," his father replied. "You've got school tomorrow."

"Yeah, like I could forget?"

Super Mufti

It's like clockwork! Tony thought when, shortly after his parents had left, there was a soft knock on his window. He happily pushed the curtains aside—and froze.

Outside on the window ledge, someone was crouched and looking at him with wide eyes. And although the figure was sitting in the dark and had pulled a cape right up to its chin, Tony could clearly tell that it was not the little vampire. Could it be Aunt Dorothee? An icy chill ran down his spine, and he quickly closed the curtains.

Then there was another knock, and a cheery voice called, "It's me, Anna!" Rudolph's little sister! Relieved, but also a little annoyed, Tony opened the window and let her in.

"Did you have to scare me like that?" he asked.

Anna smoothed out her cape and giggled. In the bright

light of his desk lamp, he noticed that her small, round face looked unusually rosy. Her hair was combed and pulled back off her face with two barrettes.

"I just wanted to check if you knew any other vampire girls," she said teasingly. "See, if you'd shouted, 'Hello, Julia,' I wouldn't have invited you to my vampire-day party."

"Vampire-day party?"

"Today is the day I became a vampire," she said proudly. "My birthday, so to speak. The only day we vampires really celebrate. Look what Rudolph gave me."

She pulled out a tattered book from under her cape and showed it to him. "It's very exciting!"

"I know," replied Tony, who knew the book very well. It was *Bloody Bites*, which he had lent to the little vampire a few weeks ago.

"Why, do you know it?" asked Anna.

"No, no," he said quickly. "It just sounds exciting."

"And I got the barrettes from Gregory," she said.

They didn't look very new, Tony thought, but at least it was nice of Gregory to give his sister something.

"And I'm wearing the best present!" she said. "But you can't see it."

"Why not?" wondered Tony.

"Just—smell."

"Oh!" So he wasn't wrong in thinking that he'd noticed a particularly pungent smell coming from Anna. "A new perfume?" he asked.

"Right!" she exclaimed. "Well, for me anyway: Super Mufti."

Tony swallowed. Mufti Eleganti, which Anna had used occasionally before, was bad enough, but Super Mufti! It reeked of smelly cheese, sweaty feet, and stink bombs.

"What else did you get?" he asked quickly, before she could ask him what he thought of the perfume.

She hesitated, and then an embarrassed smile crossed her face.

"I'll only tell you if you promise not to laugh!"

She reached under her cape and pulled out a pacifier. It was a long, already quite chewed, rubber pacifier with a dirty white mouthpiece. A black ribbon, probably a shoelace, was tied to a ring on the end of it.

Tony had to bite his tongue not to laugh. Anna with a pacifier. That was too weird!

She watched him anxiously. But when he looked at her quite seriously, his face twisted in pain because his tongue hurt, she breathed a sigh of relief.

"It's for my teeth," she explained. "Every child vampire has to use one so that our front teeth stay small, and our fangs grow nice and long."

Tony was shocked. He knew her as Anna the Toothless, who survived on milk.

"Do you have fangs?" he asked.

"Yeah," she said evasively, "small ones. But I'll use the pacifier mostly in my coffin," she quickly added, "and other times when I feel like it."

With that, she hid it under her cape again.

"But now we need to get going!" she announced.

"Where?"

"To the crypt, of course!"

"To the crypt?" exclaimed Tony, dismayed. "What for?"

"To celebrate my vampire-day," Anna said cheerfully.

He felt his heart beat faster. He liked birthday parties; they were fun. But vampire-day parties . . . ? Wouldn't they be creepy?

Maybe Anna already had vampire fangs and wanted to try them out on him in the crypt? He felt woozy and had to hold on to his desk with both hands.

"I—I can't," he replied. "I have to wait for Rudolph."

"But he's in the crypt!"

She threw him a second cape, which she had kept hidden under her own.

"Come on!" she said. "Otherwise Gregory will lose his patience."

"Gregory's gonna be there too?"

"Of course," Anna replied. "He loves vampire-day parties."

"And your o-other relatives?" asked Tony. "Aunt Dorothee and Wilhelm the Dry and Hildegard the Thirsty and Sabine the Terrible and Ludwig the Horrible?"

"They're all out."

There was a pause. Tony looked helplessly at the moth-eaten, musty-smelling cape in his hands while Anna climbed onto the windowsill.

Should he really fly off with her?

At least he could catch up with Rudolph there. Even though they had agreed to meet, Rudolph was clearly not going to come here on his sister's vampire-day. And there wasn't much time left until next Sunday. . . .

"All right," he agreed with a sigh, putting on the cape and climbing onto the windowsill with Anna. She looked at him and smiled. Then she spread her arms and floated away.

Still feeling somewhat uncertain, he followed her.

In the Air

When he put on a vampire cape and flew, Tony always had a strange lump in his stomach at first. He moved his arms up and down hesitantly and squinted down anxiously, where six floors below him, cars looked like children's toys.

But once he felt confident that the air was holding him up, his movements became stronger, his flapping more even. It was like swimming—only much easier.

"You're flying like a real vampire," said Anna, who glided quietly next to him.

"Really?" he said, grinning sheepishly.

Although she had certainly meant well, an uneasy feeling crept over him: Was he turning into a vampire?

On the other hand, he knew full well that a human

could only become a vampire from a vampire's bite. . . .

His fear that Anna might want to test her new teeth out on him once he was in the crypt rose up again, and he gave her an anxious sideward glance. She looked particularly strange in the moonlight. Her face shimmered like a white flower under her dark hair. Her lips were slightly open, and he could see her teeth, small and round like pearls. If she was really growing fangs, he couldn't see them. Maybe he was getting worried for nothing.

"Watch out!" Anna shocked him out of his reverie.

He just barely missed flying into a chimney looming up in front of them. He managed to dodge around it at the last second.

"You need to watch where you're going," Anna reproached him. "The air is full of dangers. Look there, for example. It's Aunt Dorothee."

"W-what?" stuttered Tony. Frightened, he forgot to move his arms. Anna grabbed his cape before he fell out of the sky.

"She's off to a fireman's ball," she reassured him. "That's what she told me, anyway."

He let out a sigh of relief. Now he could be sure there was no risk of Aunt Dorothee showing up unexpectedly in the crypt while they were celebrating Anna's vampire-day!

Ahead of them was the old, weather-beaten cemetery wall that ran around the abandoned rear part of the cemetery, where crosses and gravestones lay on the ground in knee-high grass and where visitors rarely wandered. This was where the Sackville-Bagg family had built their underground crypt to keep themselves safe from Ravenhood, the cemetery caretaker who was stalking them.

Anna flew slowly along the wall, searching intently through the darkness.

Tony, who kept his distance while following her, asked in a whisper, "Do you see Ravenhood?"

She shook her head. "He's probably in his house carving wooden stakes," she said bitterly.

They flew over the wall and landed in front of a tall fir

tree. Anna quickly picked up a moss-covered stone hidden in the shelter of the fir tree. It was the entrance to the crypt.

"Come on," she whispered to Tony, as she disappeared into a narrow shaft. Tony slid in behind her and pulled the stone back over the hole.

Deadbeats

The smell of decay and Super Mufti greeted them. It was so strong Tony nearly choked. With weak knees, he groped his way down the steps behind Anna. His heart was in his mouth.

Why had he been so stupid as to come along? Surely there would have been another opportunity to talk to Rudolph. Down here he was at Gregory's mercy—Gregory and all the other vampires who could come back at any moment. . . . Or maybe they were already waiting for him?

But in the candlelight, he only saw Gregory and Rudolph lying in their coffins. The other coffins were closed.

Tony breathed a sigh of relief. So it was true that the

rest of the family was out flying around. Nevertheless, he thought he'd better be careful, so he stopped on the last step, where he was in the dark.

Anna ran to the two open coffins and shouted indignantly, "You deadbeats! You promised you'd prepare everything for my vampire-day party!"

Rudolph rose from his coffin and looked remorseful. "My book was too exciting," he said.

"And Gregory?"

"He fell asleep."

"And my vampire-day party? I thought you wanted to put the coffins together and decorate the crypt."

"We did," said Rudolph meekly, "and we started doing it."

"And?"

"Gregory felt faint and had to lie down."

"His usual stunt!" scolded Anna. "What'll Tony think of us now?"

"Tony?" asked Rudolph, surprised. "Is he here?"

"Yes," said Tony, and took a few hesitant steps into the

crypt. "But I can go home right away," he offered. "Don't go out of your way for my sake."

"That would be just great!" exclaimed Anna angrily. "No, you're staying. Invited is invited. Come on, Rudolph, we have to wake up Gregory!"

"Wake up Gregory?" Rudolph looked at her in shock. "You know what he's like when he's disturbed from his sleep!"

"I'm already awake!" growled a hoarse voice, as Gregory's pale face emerged from the coffin. "With all the noise you were making." His deep-set eyes were half-closed. "You clearly have not heard of consideration for others," he hissed.

Rudolph hurried over to help him get out of his coffin.

"It's only because it's Anna's vampire-day," Rudolph told Gregory soothingly, "and because of Tony."

"Tony?" Now Gregory was wide awake. His penetrating gaze fell on Tony, who felt a shiver run down his spine.

"How could I forget!" exclaimed Gregory, his voice suddenly sounding very friendly. "Our guest!" Smiling broadly, he approached Tony, grabbed him, and croaked, "Welcome!"

Tony had turned deadly pale. Welcome—that could only mean one thing: blood!

A Predator's Claws

But escape was out of the question: Gregory was much taller and stronger than Tony, and his hands held him like a vise.

Tony could now see Gregory up close. His white face with its red dimples on his chin and the tip of his nose, the ominously glowing eyes with dark shadows underneath, and his wide mouth with its bright white, protruding fangs. He could smell Gregory's deadly breath—it was worse than Super Mufti!

He was about to faint, he could tell, when Anna stepped up next to Gregory and tugged at his cape, saying, "If you're so happy to see Tony, prove it and rearrange the crypt for him."

"Rearrange the crypt?" said Gregory. "That's a lot of work."

He looked at Tony intensely.

"Lazy bum," said Anna, but so quietly that Gregory graciously ignored it.

"That's a nice sweater," he said to Tony. "Pure wool, isn't it?"

"I—I don't know," Tony stammered, taking a step backward.

Gregory held him by the sweater, pretending to check the material. "Or is it synthetic? Let me guess, forty percent wool, sixty percent synthetic. Am I right?"

With a strong jerk he pulled Tony toward him and pushed down his collar, exposing Tony's neck. As if through a fog, Tony saw Gregory's head approaching . . . bending down to his neck. . . .

He cried out in horror.

Gregory immediately let go.

"What's with you?" he growled. "I just wanted to check the label on the back of your sweater."

He stomped back to his coffin and sat down on the edge.

"By the way, I was right," he said. "Forty percent wool and sixty percent synthetic."

With that, he pulled a nail file out from under his pillow and began to file the long, curved nails of his left hand. Tony's scalp bristled at the sight of these predatory claws.

Gregory seemed completely absorbed in his task, an ecstatic smile on his lips as again and again he paused to look at his even sharper nails.

"You can start anytime, by the way," he said in a soft voice, so busy with what he was doing that he didn't even raise his head.

"Doing what?" asked Anna.

"Rearranging the crypt."

"But—" Anna started to protest, but Rudolph threw her an exasperated look and shook his head vigorously. He quickly walked over to the five coffins that stood on the left wall and set about pushing them together to form a seating area. Gritting her teeth, Anna helped.

"Sh-shall I help?" asked Tony.

"No, thanks," said Anna, "but—"

"But who?" answered Gregory.

"Me, of course," Tony said instantly. *Anything to not provoke Gregory!* he thought. He went over to the foot of the last coffin, which had to be very heavy, because Anna and Rudolph were only able to move it with great difficulty. With horror he realized that it was Aunt Dorothee's coffin. What if she was in it?

Anna had noticed his worried look and said quietly, "The family treasure is in here. Aunt Dorothee guards it like a hawk. Whenever she leaves, she always puts the chest in her coffin."

"And the treasure is that heavy?"

"Of course. It's solid gold jewelry and coins and other valuables!"

"Do vampires wear jewelry?" Tony asked.

"If they want to look attractive for someone, they do.

Also, we keep it for funds. When things get tough, we exchange some of the valuables for cash. Vampires can't set up bank accounts."

"Hey, what are you two whispering about?" It was Gregory's gravelly voice. "You're talking about me, I bet."

"No, no," said Anna quickly. "We were discussing the seating arrangement. So, two coffins as a table and the other three as benches. Right?"

"Only three as benches? But there are four of us!" Gregory said. Then he exclaimed joyfully, "Of course! Tony and I are sharing a coffin!"

"Oh no!" cried Tony.

"Why not?" asked Gregory. He turned to Tony, having put the nail file back in his coffin. "Am I supposed to guess?"

"I'd r-rather sit next to Anna," Tony stuttered. "A-after all, it's her vampire-day."

"If you want," said Gregory angrily, and climbed back into his coffin. "I wasn't done with my nails anyway."

Once again, the space was filled with the scratching

sound of the nail file.

"All the better," said Anna snappily. "At least now, every-one has a coffin to themselves. Come on, Tony!"

Food and Drink

Anna put her hand on his arm and led him over to the sitting area.

"Now let's make ourselves comfortable," she said cheerfully—as if he could ever be comfortable twelve feet underground and in the company of the unpredictable Gregory!

Anxious, Tony sat down on the coffin closest to the exit to the crypt. Anna sat on the coffin next to his.

"I bet you're thirsty," she said. "From what I've heard, there's always plenty to eat and drink at birthday parties."

"Uh-huh," agreed Tony.

"You see!" she yelled out to Rudolph, who was leaning against the wall, reading his book. Startled, he dropped the book.

"Luckily, I still have the drinks," she sighed. "Could you please bring them out, Rudolph?"

"D-drinks?" stuttered Tony. What could there be to drink at a vampire-day party? With a shudder, he imagined transparent glass bottles filled to the brim with blood. . . .

But it was small cartons of milk and chocolate milk that Rudolph put down in front of him on one of the coffins they were using as a table. There were more than twenty of them in three rather grubby shopping bags that had been stored at the foot of Anna's coffin.

"Well, what do you say about that?" asked Anna proudly.

Speechless, Tony stared at the many cartons, enough to fill a small dairy shop.

"I . . . ," he mumbled. *I'm not thirsty,* he wanted to add, but decided not to say anything, so he wouldn't upset Anna.

She pulled out a crushed straw from one of the shopping bags, jabbed it into the foil-covered hole of one of the mini chocolate-milk cartons, and handed the carton cheerfully to Tony.

"Try it!"

"Th-thanks."

He took it reluctantly. Despite the label claiming CHOCOLATE DRINK, ALWAYS TASTY AND DELICIOUS, it didn't look very appetizing. On the contrary, the carton was covered with a thin layer of dust, and its corners were rather crushed.

"What about you?" he asked. "Aren't you going to drink anything?"

Anna and Rudolph exchanged glances and giggled.

"Anna doesn't drink milk anymore," explained Rudolph.

"No more milk?" said Tony. "But—"

"And no more chocolate milk either," added Rudolph.

"Then who are all these cartons for?"

"You," Anna replied.

"All of them?"

"Well," said Anna, smiling bashfully. "Originally, they were for me, but now—"

She didn't finish, but quickly turned her head away. Tony noticed that she had blushed a deep red.

Then he remembered the pacifier she was supposed to use to grow nice long fangs. So she had become . . . a true vampire!

He felt the carton in his hand tremble. And the vampires noticed it too. Suddenly they all seemed to be staring at him. Even Gregory had stopped filing his nails.

"Why don't you try it?" he shouted, his voice sounding threatening.

"I—I will," stammered Tony, and sucked on the straw. He almost spat it out again—it was disgusting. It tasted like soap! But then he noticed the vampires looking at him expectantly.

"It's really d-delicious," he lied.

"You see!" growled Gregory.

"Anna's been keeping them for you for a while now!" Rudolph added.

Anna smiled proudly. "Now I don't need them anymore." Then she added, "Just let me know when you're done, okay? I'll get you another one."

Tony nodded weakly. Just the thought of having to

drink any more of the awful stuff made him nauseous. He had already planned on how he was going to avoid drinking more: he was just going to pretend he was drinking from the carton he had and make it last all evening.

Anna stood up, smoothed out her cape, and brushed the hair off her face.

"And now," she said, "since we've finished eating and drinking, the fun can begin!"

Coffin Hopping

"Yes!" cried Gregory eagerly, and clambered out of his coffin. "What game should we play first?"

"Yes, what do you suggest?" Anna turned to Tony and looked at him questioningly. "What games do you usually play at birthday parties?"

Tony hesitated. Under certain circumstances, a harmless game could become life-threatening if played with vampires in a crypt. It definitely couldn't be a game where the candles would have to be blown out—there was no telling what Gregory might do in the dark. Nor any hiding games—because that could mean that Tony would have to crawl into a coffin!

"A sack race," he said at last.

"A sack race?" Anna wrinkled her nose. "Sounds boring."

"I think so too," agreed Rudolph. "Besides, we don't have any sacks."

"Wait a minute," said Gregory. "That's giving me an idea . . . Sack races, sack races . . . I've got it: coffin hopping!"

"Coffin hopping?" Anna still didn't sound very enthusiastic.

"Yes! We line up the coffins with different distances between them, and then we have to jump from coffin to coffin without falling. Whoever does it, wins!"

"Is that all?" said Anna grumpily.

"Just wait and see!"

Gregory put the lids on his and Rudolph's coffins. Then he started to set up the obstacle course: first his own coffin, which was decorated with a *G* with a two-headed dragon wrapped around it. Then Rudolph's, then Anna's—neither of theirs had anything on them and were much smaller than Gregory's. At the end of the course, he placed a large coffin with golden handles on the sides. Tony thought he remembered it to be the coffin belonging to Gregory, Rudolph, and Anna's mother—Hildegard the Thirsty. The first two coffins were quite close together, Tony thought. The distance between the second and third coffins was greater, and the one between Anna's and Hildegard's coffins seemed huge to him.

"I'll never be able to jump that," he mumbled.

"You don't always have to win," Gregory said venomously.

He pulled out a box of matches from under his cape, took out three matchsticks, and broke off a different-length piece from each one. Then he put the sticks between the fingers of his left hand so that they all looked the same length.

"You choose first," he said, nodding to Tony. After everyone except Gregory had taken one, they compared the lengths of their matches. Rudolph had the shortest one, so he went first.

He easily made the jump from the first to the second

coffin. But during the second jump he got caught up in his cape and fell to the ground.

He got up slowly and tried the last jump, but he didn't make it. He fell against the side of Hildegard's coffin. Dragging his right leg and even paler than usual, he limped back to the others.

"One point," Gregory announced. Now it was Tony's turn. He jumped effortlessly from Gregory's to Rudolph's coffin. The jump to Anna's coffin was harder, but he managed it.

"Bravo, Tony!" cheered Anna.

"Shhhh!" said Gregory darkly. "No encouragement allowed!"

Only one coffin left . . . Tony took a deep breath and jumped. His knees hit the side.

"Ouch!" he cried.

Wincing in pain, he limped back to the start.

"Two points," said Gregory.

Now it was Anna's turn. In her wide, far-too-long cape,

which reached almost to her ankles, she looked tiny and fragile. Tony felt his heart beat faster—for her!

She jumped, light as a feather. She easily managed the first two obstacles. "Take care!" Tony wanted to cry out, as she leapt into the air. She landed on the last coffin—and slipped off.

"Too bad," Gregory said. "Two points, like Tony."

Anna walked back with her head held high.

"And I am the smallest!" she said proudly. In the meantime, Gregory had climbed onto his coffin and did a few knee bends to loosen up. Compared to Anna, he was enormously tall and strong, not to mention broad-shouldered, with muscular calves. No wonder he jumped easily from coffin to coffin. When he reached the last coffin, he threw up his arms and bragged, "Gregory, the greatest coffin hopper ever!"

"Cheater," grumbled Anna.

"Did you say something?" Gregory asked her, staring ominously as usual.

"No, no," Anna said quickly.

"Anna just said that you jump well," Rudolph assured him.

"Don't I?" Gregory stretched and took a deep breath. "It's thanks to my diet and lifestyle. . . ."

He stared unconsciously at Tony's neck and bared his terrifying teeth.

"Hey!" cried Anna. "It's time for another game, Gregory!"

Gregory flinched. Reluctantly, he averted his gaze.

"Which one?" he asked unkindly.

Oink, Piggy, Oink

"I know one," said Rudolph.

"You do?" said Gregory incredulously.

"Yeah."

"What's it called?"

"Oink, piggy, oink."

"Beep, beep!" Gregory tapped his forehead. "You made it up."

"No, he didn't," said Tony. "It's a real game."

"And how do you know about it?" Gregory asked Rudolph.

"Well—" Rudolph put on a serious face and cleared his throat. "The children sat in a circle—"

"Which children?"

"The children in the room that looked so warm and

cozy from outside. I was freezing and hungry as I sat on the window ledge, watching them. A kid with a blindfold stood in the middle of the circle. He spun around a few times, then sat down so that he landed on another kid's lap. 'Oink, piggy, oink!' he said. And then the kid whose lap he was sitting on oinked loudly, and the blindfolded kid had to guess whose lap he was sitting on."

Gregory seemed to like the sound of the game, because a smile spread across his face. "Doesn't sound so bad, your 'oink, piggy, oink,'" he said. "But I'm in the middle!"

He reached under his cape and pulled out a black cloth. It was full of moth holes.

"B-but you can see through that," Tony mumbled.

"So?" hissed Gregory. "You don't want me to get it wrong, do you?"

"N-no. It's just that the rules of the game—"

"Pah, rules!" said Gregory, swatting away any further objections with a wave of his hand. "Just blindfold me."

"Okay," said Rudolph. He climbed up onto a coffin and quickly knotted the cloth behind Gregory's head. It hung down and covered his face as well as his eyes.

"We can start now," growled Gregory.

"All right." Rudolph struggled to push the two coffins that had served as a table against the wall. Anna stood and watched and smiled mockingly.

"You're letting him boss you around," she said to Rudolph.

"What're you talking about?" Gregory said. "He's the one who suggested the game, isn't he?"

His voice sounded muffled and scary through the cloth. Rudolph gestured wildly to Anna not to argue with Gregory, but Anna pretended not to understand.

"You could have helped him," she said to Gregory. "After all, you're the strongest."

"True!" said Gregory. "But that doesn't mean that I should have to do all the hard work. Besides, if you continue to pick on me, I'll tell Aunt Dorothee that Tony was here."

"What?" said Tony. He looked at Anna in horror, but she shook her head very slightly.

"Empty threats," she whispered.

Pleased with the effect his words had had, Gregory took a few cautious steps.

"Are you ready?" he asked.

Anna and Tony quickly sat down on Aunt Dorothee's coffin. Rudolph sat down on the middle coffin. Gregory slowly approached them. He looked scary, as all that was visible was the moth-eaten cloth under his shaggy mane of hair and his powerful hairy forearms sticking out from under his wide cape. He held his hands outstretched and moved his long, bony fingers up and down—as though he was struggling to find his way around. But Anna, Rudolph, and Tony knew that he could see through the holes in the cloth!

At first it seemed as if he was going to sit on Rudolph's lap. Tony was just breathing a sigh of relief when Gregory staggered past Rudolph and stopped in front of him. Then he turned around and sat on Tony's lap.

Tony thought he was going to suffocate. Gregory was so heavy, and the smell coming off him was unbearable.

"Oink, piggy, oink!"

"Oink!" Tony cried.

"Louder!"

"Oink!" squeaked Tony.

"It's Tony!" Gregory shouted, tearing the cloth off his face and looking triumphantly around the group. "Have I won something?"

"No. But you get to blindfold Tony now," instructed Rudolph.

"Is that all?" grumbled Gregory. Angry, he wrapped the cloth around Tony's head and started tying it. Suddenly he let out a scream. It was such a bloodcurdling cry that an ice-cold shudder ran down Tony's spine.

"My fingernail!" he shrieked. "It broke!"

He stared, stunned, at his left index finger.

"My longest, most beautiful nail! I've been pampering it for weeks! I was so proud of it! And now look," he sobbed, glaring at Tony bitterly. "And it's all your fault!"

"My fault?"

"Yes, your head's fault!" the vampire roared. "Your

noodle, your noggin, your nut, your stupid, stupid skull!"

He ran to his coffin, took out the nail file, and began to fiercely file his nail.

"It's your own fault if you can't tie a knot with your nails," Anna said.

"What?" thundered Gregory. "Is that the thanks I get for staying in here just to celebrate your vampire-day? Well, that's the final straw!"

Snorting with rage, he threw the nail file back into the coffin and stomped off toward the exit.

"Big brothers should be outlawed!" Anna called after him. But Gregory didn't answer. The others heard the scrape of the stone—then everything was quiet.

Rules Are Rules

"He's spoiled everything!" scolded Anna.

"Why did you have to argue with him?" Rudolph asked.

"Why?" exclaimed Anna. "Because I don't like bullies. That's why!"

"The three of us could still celebrate," Tony suggested timidly, trying to placate the two of them. *And without Gregory, it might actually be fun. . . .*

But Anna shook her head decisively. "No!" She pulled the barrettes out of her hair and stuffed them angrily under her cape. "I wanna go to the movies."

"To the movies?" said Tony, surprised. "But most of them have already started, and besides, they don't let children in alone this late anyway."

Anna defiantly pushed out her lower lip.

"Then what about a dance club!"

"But—" Tony began. He was about to say, "We can't get in there, either," but that would have made Anna even angrier.

"I haven't got any money," he said quickly.

"Money? No problem!" She went over to Aunt Dorothee's coffin, took off the lid, and revealed an old, worm-eaten chest. Anna opened it and pulled out a few gold coins. They sparkled and glistened in the candlelight, almost taking Tony's breath away.

"Is this enough?" she asked.

But before Tony could answer, Rudolph walked over and took the gold pieces from Anna. "That's against the rules!" he roared. "The gold pieces are only for emergencies."

"But this is an emergency!" cried Anna. "First you ruin my vampire-day celebration, and then, when I want to go to a dance club so that I can do at least *one* fun thing to celebrate, you won't let me have a few measly old gold coins!"

"Rules are rules," replied Rudolph, putting the coins back into the chest and shutting it carefully.

Then he slid the lid back over Dorothee's coffin. Anna shook her fists at him angrily. "You, you . . . camel!"

Rudolph smiled. "Camel? How cute!"

"You uncivilized oaf! You brute!" Tears poured from her eyes.

She quickly spun around and ran toward the exit.

"I've had enough," she cried. "I'm going!"

"Anna," said Tony, worried.

"Rudolph can take you home," she sobbed. Then she was gone.

It's Different for Us Vampires

A cold breeze blew through the crypt, making the candles flicker. Tony shivered. It suddenly occurred to him that his parents had only gone out for a walk. Maybe they were already back and had noticed that he wasn't in his bed?

"You—you will take me back, w-won't you?" he asked anxiously.

"If you can wait a little," said the little vampire. He went over to his coffin, took off the lid, and lay down in it. "I need to rest a little after that exhausting party."

"But I really need to go home *now*!" protested Tony.

The vampire yawned. "You can't be in that much of a hurry." He took out his book and flipped through it until he found the right page. "This story about Mrs. Lunt is so exciting," he gushed. "I'm just at the part where the man sits down in the armchair and notices the smell—" He giggled. "Do you know what he was smelling?"

Of course Tony knew the story. It was from Hugh Walpole's *All Souls' Night*. The smell came from Mrs. Lunt, who had been dead for a year. But he shook his head anyway.

"I forgot."

"I never forget what I've read," boasted the vampire.

"But you do forget to return books."

"What? Which ones?"

"*Bloody Bites*. You even gave it to Anna, even though it's mine!"

"I only lent it to her."

"Anna said you gave it to her for her vampire-day."

"So? Tomorrow her vampire-day is over, and I can take it back."

"But you gave it to her—"

"It's different for us vampires."

"Well, that's pretty mean!" said Tony. Even if he was

going to make Rudolph mad, he could not keep quiet about something so unfair. But the vampire just stroked the page in his book, looking bored.

"Could you let me read in peace now?" he grumbled.

"Now wait a minute," Tony said, raising his voice. Now he was about to find out if the little vampire was a real friend or not. "We need to talk about the vacation plans."

The vampire's expression quickly changed. His grumpy look vanished and he started to smile. He said softly, "What's left to talk about? It's all arranged."

"What do you mean?" asked Tony, surprised.

"I mean, I've decided to go with you."

Tony was speechless for a second.

Then he yelled, "You're really coming too? Oh, Rudolph!" In his excitement, he spread his arms and ran toward the vampire. "You're a real friend!"

"Yup, I am!" The vampire smiled smugly. "Unlike Gregory, who's only invited George to stay in the crypt."

"George who?"

"George the Quick-Tempered. The one who won the Best Fragrance Prize at the vampire ball."

"Oh." Tony could well remember the bald, heavyset vampire who had strolled across the stage, conceited and puffed-up while getting sniffed by the judges.

"Didn't he win a blanket for his coffin?" he asked.

"That's right!" said the little vampire, gritting his teeth. He went over to Gregory's coffin and pulled out a black silk cloth. "But he gave it to Gregory, who was complaining that his feet were always cold."

"Gave it to him?" Tony grinned. "Lent it, then! It's different for you vampires. . . ."

But Rudolph didn't catch his sarcasm. With a grim look on his face, he pulled a watch chain, a cigarette case, a tiepin with a pearl, and a pocket comb out of Gregory's coffin.

"Here! All of these are from George the Quick-Tempered. To thank him, Gregory invited him to stay in the crypt for a whole week, starting Saturday night, even though I told him that I absolutely did not want to cross paths with George the Quick-Tempered under any circumstances."

"Why not?" asked Tony.

"Because he could recognize me."

Tony shook his head uncomprehendingly.

"And why shouldn't he?"

"Six weeks ago," the vampire began, "I was flying back to the cemetery when I saw a young man, clearly full of blood, walking down the street. I hadn't had much to eat yet, and my stomach immediately started grumbling. So I landed a few steps behind him and sneaked up to him. Suddenly a loud roar came out of the bushes next to me. It was George the Quick-Tempered, who had been lurking there and saw me about to snatch his prey away from him. Furious, he went for me. I ran. George chased me. Before he could catch me, however, he slipped on a pile of dog poo and fell flat on his face. I quickly squeezed through a gap in the hedge but could hear George yelling after me, 'One of these nights, I will find you and pummel you!'" The little vampire broke off and stared gloomily in front of him.

Tony, on the other hand, had to bite his lip so as not to show his delight.

He had expected many reactions—the vampire's usual indifference, his endless sighs and complaints, a hundred excuses—but not that he would easily agree to come along. And not only that, his fear of George the Quick-Tempered would ensure that he wouldn't change his mind, because he had to hide somewhere. Now, there was just the problem of how to get the vampire and his coffin to Little Ol' Molting.

But the vampire seemed to have thought about that, too.

"We need to go by train," he said. "You bring me some of your clothes to wear, and then we'll travel like two normal people. I've always wanted to travel by train and not just fly over them."

"And your c-coffin?"

"We'll wrap it in packing paper." The vampire giggled.

"Do you even know if there are any trains that go to Little Ol' Molting?" asked Tony.

"Aren't there?" the vampire exclaimed.

"There probably aren't even any tracks that run into that Podunk town," said Tony.

The vampire looked heartbroken.

"I hadn't thought of that," he mumbled.

But then his eyes lit up again. "Then we'll get off at the closest station there is. So you need to find out about train schedules and stations."

"Me?" said Tony. "We! You're coming with me to Little Ol' Molting."

"True, but nobody will give a vampire that sort of information," Rudolph replied meekly.

"Then we'll fly to get the information together," said Tony.

Strange Behavior

Half an hour later, after they had visited the station, Tony and the little vampire landed at the top of the chestnut tree in front of Tony's building.

"Your window's open," whispered the vampire, who could see much better in the dark than Tony could.

"I really hope my parents aren't back yet," Tony mumbled.

Just then the front door opened. Tony recognized Mrs. Washman, with her fat dachshund Susi on a leash. Susi stopped, raised her muzzle, and sniffed. Then she began to bark.

"Shhhh!" hissed Mrs. Washman.

But Susi continued to bark and tugged at the leash: she wanted to go to the chestnut tree!

The little vampire slid restlessly back and forth on his branch.

"I think I'd better fly off," he grumbled, and added insistently, "Don't forget, Saturday at the old cemetery wall. And bring some of your clothes!"

"And you, your coffin!" replied Tony.

The little vampire spread out his cape and flew away.

Mrs. Washman looked up anxiously at the apartment windows in the building, and then she pulled Susi to the bushes around the playground. When she had gone, Tony flew into his room and closed the window behind him. He could see light under his door. Had his parents come back already? Or had they forgotten to turn off the lights?

He quickly pulled the vampire cape over his head and hid it in the closet under his Austrian lederhosen, and the matching traditional jacket that his grandmother had knitted for him—neither of which he ever wore. Then he listened. Wasn't that his mother's voice in the kitchen? He opened his door a crack so he could hear what they were saying.

"And I'm telling you, he's not in his bed!" His mother sounded worried.

"Then he's in the bathroom," his father said.

"No! I looked in there."

"Then he must have crawled into our bed."

"No! He's not in our bedroom, either."

"Then you must not have really looked."

"Not really looked!" his mother said indignantly. "Go see for yourself, then."

"All right!"

Tony heard his father push the chair back and stand up. In one move, Tony jumped into his bed and pulled the blanket up to his chin.

Almost immediately afterward he heard his bedroom door open.

"Well, look at that!" his father whispered. "In bed, fast asleep."

His mother walked into the room and stopped by the bed. Although Tony's eyes were shut tight, he could tell that his mother was looking him up and down. But his shoes, jeans, and sweater were well covered!

"Strange," said his mother. She hesitated. "I could have sworn the bed was empty."

"It's easy to make that mistake."

"And the window—it was open . . ."

"He could have quickly gotten up and closed it and gone back to sleep."

Tony had to bite his tongue not to laugh. His mother was much more suspicious than his father!

Fortunately for Tony, his mother's primary concern was that he was missing, but now that that was clearly not the case, she relaxed and didn't say anything more. But Tony could tell she was still bothered by it all.

His father headed out the door. Tony's mother followed him, closing the door behind her. Then, halfway down the hall, she stopped. "His clothes aren't on the chair!"

Tony's heart skipped a beat. What would happen if they came back and discovered that he was in bed, fully dressed?

His father laughed. "Maybe he put them in the laundry basket for once!"

"Maybe. He has been acting strange lately." And they both walked down the hall, chortling.

Their footsteps moved down the hall, and the TV went on.

Relieved, Tony got up, turned on his desk lamp, and undressed. He put his shoes in the closet and his sweater and pants in the laundry basket, just in case his mother came back to check. He put on his pajamas, turned off the light, and got back into bed comfortably under the covers. Now he could think more clearly about what the man at the railway ticket office had said.

At the Station

While the little vampire had hidden outside under a fir tree, Tony had walked through the fortunately deserted station hall to the ticket office.

"Hello, little man," said the man behind the counter.

"I would like some information," Tony explained in a determined voice, swallowing his anger at being referred to as "little man."

"And what is it that you would like to know?"

"What time the trains to Little Ol' Molting are next Saturday."

"Lemme look that up. Morning or afternoon?"

"Evening is best. Around nine."

The man typed on his keyboard. "What's the name of the place?"

"Little Ol' Molting."

He shook his head. "There's no train station there."

"There isn't?" Tony turned very pale. "But I need to go there!"

"Maybe you can get off at a nearby town. Do you have any names?"

"Big Ol' Molting."

Again, the man tapped on his keyboard. He looked up with a smile and said, "You're in luck! There's a train for Big Ol' Molting that leaves at eight forty-two at night and arrives at nine thirty-five. But isn't that a bit too late for you?"

"Too late? N-no. My brother is taking me."

"Oh. Is he older than you?"

"Much older," Tony giggled.

"Then everything *should* be fine," the man said.

Tony thanked him and headed toward the exit, quietly mumbling the departure and arrival times to himself so he wouldn't forget. Shortly before he reached the exit, he stopped. What could the man have meant by "Then everything *should* be fine"? Had the little vampire over-looked something in their travel preparations—something that could happen to them on an evening train? Maybe he'd better ask. So he headed back to the ticket office.

"I bet you forgot the departure and arrival time," the man said kindly. "Here, I wrote them down for you."

"Thank you," Tony said, surprised. He put the note in his pocket. "Actually, I wanted to ask you something else."

"Yes?"

"What did you mean earlier when you said, 'Then everything *should* be fine'?"

"I was just worried about what could happen if two little kids like you traveled alone on a train at night."

"What do you mean?" asked Tony.

"Well, first of all, the conductor would be suspicious."

"Why?"

"The two of you could be running away from home, for example."

Dismayed, Tony was silent. He and Rudolph hadn't thought of that at all!

"But there's no need to worry," said the man.

"Why?"

"Your big brother is going with you."

"He's not bigger," Tony replied gloomily. "Just older."

"Over eighteen?"

"Uh-huh."

"Well, you see! Then everything's fine. All your older brother needs to do is bring his ID."

"His I-ID?" stuttered Tony.

"So he can prove his age."

"Oh right, okay."

Confused, Tony made his way out to the fir tree.

"Everything all right?" the little vampire asked.

"Do you have an ID card?"

"What's an ID card?"

"A document with your name and the date you were bor—"

"I do!" the vampire interrupted him.

"Really?"

"Of course!"

A great weight fell from Tony's shoulders. "Then make sure you bring it with you on Saturday, okay!"

"Sure," said the vampire. "It's in the coffin anyway."

Tony sighed deeply. Then his eyes closed and he fell asleep.

He didn't notice his mother coming into the room and staring at his clothes in the hamper, stunned.

Packing

"You seem really tense," said Tony's mother at breakfast the next Saturday.

"I do?" responded Tony. He was actually, strangely—but not because of the suitcases that were about to be packed, nor the farm he and his parents were heading off to the next morning. It was the train ride with the little vampire that night, and the flight back afterwards, that were giving him a sick feeling in the pit of his stomach. Not even the fresh rolls that his father had brought back from the bakery tasted good to him.

"You have to eat something, Tony!"

"Okay." Listlessly, he spread butter on a roll. He bit off a small piece and chewed.

"You're not sick, are you?" asked his mother.

"No!" he exclaimed.

His parents wanted to go to the movies that night, before their week in Little Ol' Molting. But if they thought he was sick, they would probably stay home. And he could *not* let that happen, no matter what!

"I'm just a little tired," he said, hastily shoving half the roll into his mouth. "May I have two more?"

"Of course!"

After breakfast, he lay on his bed with a stomachache.

"Tony, are you packing yet?" his father asked.

"Yes," he said in a weak voice.

"Don't forget your bathing suit!"

"I won't."

Tony stood up slowly. The way he felt reminded him of the wolf in the fairy tale with the seven goats after they had filled his stomach with stones: "What rumbles and tumbles against my poor bones?"

He put his suitcase on the bed and began to pack some of his favorite books: *The Twelve Scariest Vampire Stories Ever, In the House of Count Dracula, More Vampire*

Stories. Then he put underwear, socks, two T-shirts with long sleeves, two sweaters, pajamas, and his bathing suit on top.

"I'm finished!" he shouted loudly.

"Finished?" his mother repeated from the bathroom. "That was pretty quick. You've probably forgotten half the things you'll need!"

"No, I haven't!" he shouted back defiantly, zipping up his suitcase.

He heard his mother crossing the hallway. She entered the room with what Tony knew as her I-know-better smile.

She eyed the closed suitcase. "You can't have packed much," she said.

"Enough," Tony assured her.

"Pajamas?"

"Yes."

"Underwear?"

"Yes."

"Long pants?" she asked. Without waiting for Tony's answer, she went to the closet and looked inside.

"Ugh, it smells so musty in here," she grumbled. "You need to air out your closet, Tony!"

Tony suppressed a giggle. He knew where the smell was coming from: Rudolph's cape, which was hidden under his lederhosen!

Then Tony's mother saw the new jeans that were still hanging on their hanger.

"Why didn't you pack these?" she asked.

"I—I forgot them," Tony stuttered.

"You see! You did forget something. It's a good thing I checked!"

"Yes," Tony grumbled. He couldn't possibly tell her that he had deliberately left them out because he wanted to bring them to the little vampire that evening.

"All right, then we'll put them in now," his mother said while she opened the suitcase and put the trousers inside.

"Did you remember socks?" she asked, looking at Tony's clothes in the suitcase.

"Yes!" snapped Tony, who felt that he was about to explode with anger. "You're always snooping in my things!

And now what am I gonna give Rudolph—" Horrified, he slapped his hand over his mouth. He had almost spilled the beans!

His mother looked at him curiously. "I hope you weren't planning on lending your new jeans to someone at school."

"No, I—I mean, y-yes," he stammered. "We—we were gonna swap." That wasn't true, but he needed a good reason. "He was gonna break them in for me." He added boldly, "Because I don't like jeans when they're new."

"You're perfectly capable of breaking them in yourself!" his mother scolded, shaking her head disapprovingly. "I think I'd better take your suitcase with me. Otherwise, you'll pack your scary books. And you won't relax at all while we're away!"

Decided, she zipped the bag closed, locked it, and put the key in her pocket.

"But, Mom," protested Tony.

"Too late," she said with a smile, and walked to the door with the suitcase. Tony was thinking that maybe he could say that he had forgotten to pack his thick Norwegian sweater so that she had to open the suitcase again. But then he realized that she'd be standing next to him, so he wouldn't be able to pull out the jeans for Rudolph without her noticing.

Rats! Fortunately, he hadn't packed *Dracula*, the book he was reading. He took it off the shelf and stretched out on his bed and opened it.

Soon the events taking place on the ship from Varna that was carrying Count Dracula's boxes to England had so engrossed him that he forgot everything else—the jeans, the locked suitcase, even the unsolved problem of what pants the little vampire would wear that evening.

Eternal Optimist

At half past seven, Tony's father was fully dressed and waiting in the hallway. He wore his dark green corduroy suit, green shirt, and yellow tie.

"Darling, how long will you be?" he called impatiently.

"Five more minutes," his mother replied from the bathroom.

"You're all dressed up," said Tony, leaning against his bedroom door. "Just to go to the movies?"

"We're going dancing afterward," his father explained.

Tony's heart jumped with joy. That would mean that they certainly wouldn't be home before midnight! But, of course, he couldn't let his father notice how well that fit into his plans.

"So you'll be out really late then?" he said feigning

disappointment. "You're always leaving me alone!"

"You'll keep yourself entertained, I'm sure."

"But how?"

"Watching TV, I'm guessing."

"Is that okay then?"

"Well, until ten—after all, you *are* on vacation."

"Oh, great!" he said happily. If his father only knew that tonight he would not be sitting in front of the TV, but on a train!

Tony's mother came out of the bathroom. She had on a white blouse and black velvet pants. She had curled her hair. As she put on her coat, she said to Tony, "And don't read too late, please."

"Dad said I could watch TV."

"Oh? What's on?"

"Wh-what's on?" stuttered Tony. He hadn't even looked, and since he always knew exactly what was on, his mother might get suspicious.

"A game show," he said quickly. "Quiz show, really."

"Not a scary movie?" she asked, sounding suspicious.

"No!" he assured her, smiling. Tonight he didn't need a movie to have a scary adventure!

"But at half past nine you're in bed. You'll need to be well rested for our trip tomorrow."

"Dad said ten."

"All right, ten."

It was a quarter to eight when his parents left. It was already getting dark. He had agreed to meet the little vampire at the cemetery at eight. If he hurried, he could make it in ten minutes. So he had five minutes to spare. Five minutes to find a pair of trousers for the little vampire, put the cape in a bag, and grab the tickets. . . .

Rudolph's New Clothes

Shortly after eight, Tony turned into the dark path that led to the cemetery. Thick bushes lined both sides and seemed to be stretching out their branches toward him. They crackled and creaked. Suddenly Tony screamed: something soft had dashed between his legs and, with a mournful cry, disappeared into the bushes. He began to run.

On the side of the path, half-hidden by the bushes, was a bench. Terrified, he realized that it was occupied. Someone was sitting there in the dark. Tony's heart was pounding. Could it be Aunt Dorothee?

As he came closer, he realized that there were two people on the bench—a couple embracing and not the least bit interested in him.

He hurried past. Only when he saw the old cemetery

wall in front of him did he breathe a sigh of relief. The little vampire would be waiting for him there, in the bushes.

"Rudolph?" he called.

There was rustling in the bushes, and a branch snapped. Then a small figure, wrapped in a cape, stepped onto the path.

"You?" said Tony, surprised.

"Hello, Tony," Anna said, smiling.

"I . . . ," he mumbled, searching for something to say. He knew that he couldn't ask about Rudolph straightaway, as that would anger her. He knew how sensitive she was.

"It—uh—it's great to see you," he said, hoping he sounded convincing.

"Really?" She beamed. "Greater than if it had been Rudolph?"

"Well," he said evasively. "Actually, I was supposed to meet up with him—"

"I know." She smiled. "He's waiting for you. He sent me to get you because he didn't want to leave his coffin unguarded. Come on!"

She grabbed him by the arm and led him between the bushes to the cemetery wall. There, in the shadow, was Rudolph, sitting on his coffin.

"You're late," he grumbled.

"I didn't know which pants to bring you," Tony tried to explain. "My mother packed the jeans I had planned to bring and locked the suitcase."

"So what am I gonna wear then?" growled the little vampire.

Bashfully, Tony pulled out of his tote bag the only pants he had to bring, the lederhosen. His brown corduroys were with his grandmother. She was sewing patches on the knees. The black linen ones were in the wash.

"These," Tony said, holding them up by the bib. Anna, who was standing next to him, giggled lightly. She obviously thought the lederhosen were as ridiculous as Tony did.

"I didn't have any other ones," he said apologetically.

But the little vampire seemed to like the pants. He stroked the smooth leather and embroidery with his skinny fingers.

"Pretty," he said.

Anna laughed out loud.

"You're just jealous," Rudolph snapped. "That they're for *me*! That Tony brought them with him especially for *me*!"

He quickly put them on.

Tony put his hand over his mouth so as not to laugh. With his chalk-pale face, his straggly, shoulder-length hair, the too-wide lederhosen with the embroidered bib and the suspenders sagging around his skinny frame, into which he had stuffed his cape, and then his thin legs in holey tights sticking out the bottom, the little vampire looked like a scarecrow.

Maybe the traditional matching jacket would make him look a little less frightening? Tony thought. He had packed it and the Tyrolean hat, which, in his grandmother's opinion, went so well with it, just in case. He reached into his bag and took out the jacket.

"This goes with them," he said, "if you want it."

"Oh yes!" cried the vampire. He quickly put it on. His face lit up.

"It's great!" he enthused, spinning the silver buttons, which sparkled in the moonlight.

Tony held back a laugh. Anna giggled furtively. "You look like you're going to a costume party!" she said.

"Really? You're just jealous!"

"I have something else," said Tony, pulling out the felt hat with the green feather.

The vampire was thrilled. Smiling happily, he put the hat on over his shaggy hair.

"I've always wanted a hat with a feather like this!"

He paraded a few steps around the coffin, while Anna and Tony looked at each other, trying very hard not to laugh. Compared to his "normal" vampire appearance, however, Rudolph looked rather odd, Tony thought. And that was perhaps just as well, since they were going to travel by train.

The train . . . oh no! He suddenly remembered that their train was leaving at 8:42! And with the heavy coffin, it would take at least ten minutes to get to the station.

"Our train is going to leave soon. Come on, Rudolph, hurry up!"

"Take it easy," the vampire said. "I need to adjust my hat first."

"But we'll be too late!"

"Nonsense!" growled the vampire as he clumsily adjusted his hat.

"Typical," hissed Anna. "I'll have to carry the coffin for him!"

With that, she lifted the coffin in the middle. Her small, thin legs seemed to almost buckle under the load, but she squared her narrow shoulders and set off. Tony walked beside her.

"Shouldn't I be helping?" he offered.

"No," she said with a smile. "I can do it."

"Wait!" cried the little vampire. "I can't walk that fast with this hat!"

Shipping Paper

On the way, the little vampire suddenly called out, "Stop! We still have to wrap the coffin!"

Stunned, Anna stopped and put down the coffin.

"Do you have any packing paper?" she asked.

"No. But Tony does."

Tony was shocked. "I do?"

"Yes, that's what we agreed," the vampire growled. "You were going to bring something for me to wear and the paper to wrap the coffin."

Tony shook his head vigorously. "That's not true! We only discussed bringing you something to wear."

"Didn't I say that the coffin needed to be wrapped in shipping paper?"

"Yes. But not that I should bring the paper."

"Pah!" said the vampire angrily. "So whadda we do now?"

"Maybe you can buy some paper at the station," Anna said.

"No," said Tony, "there's no paper for sale there."

"If the coffin's not wrapped, I'm not coming!" threatened the little vampire.

"With George the Quick-Tempered in the crypt?" replied Tony with a grin.

This time he wasn't going to let himself be bullied, because he knew how much the little vampire wanted to come along.

"No, no," the vampire quickly relented. "Of course I'm coming. But my coffin!" he added in a tearful voice. "If someone takes it, I'm lost!"

In the meantime, Anna had walked around the coffin, studying it from all sides.

"I don't think it looks like a coffin," she said. "More like a chest."

"Sailors have chests like that," Tony said.

"But I'm not a sailor," the vampire said miserably.

"And you don't really look like a sailor," Anna giggled, looking over his outfit with its Tyrolean hat.

"But you could still have a box like this," said Tony. "And now, we really need to get going. We don't want to miss the train!"

He and Anna carried the coffin together the rest of the way to the brightly lit station.

"I hope everything's gonna be okay!" whined the little vampire, who followed them on shaky legs. He was so scared that he hadn't even noticed that his hat was lopsided.

"Could you at least ask?" he implored Tony after they had put the coffin down behind a bush.

"Ask what?"

"If they sell packing paper. There are always shops in train stations."

Tony looked at the large station clock. It was eight twenty-three.

"All right. But don't get your hopes up."

Disgruntled, because he had let himself be persuaded, he went into the station. Why would a kiosk be open so late? Late last Sunday, all the shops had been closed.

In the station hall, his eyes first fell on two women standing at the ticket office. They wore long green coats, Tyrolean hats, and hiking boots. He had to smile; they matched Rudolph's outfit perfectly. If they end up in the same car, one might think they were traveling together! Then he saw that the small kiosk on the other side of the hall was lit up. A man sat behind the open window.

"Do you have packing paper?" asked Tony.

"I used to have some," the man answered, "but whether I still do . . ."

He opened a drawer, looked inside, and shook his head.

"It's sold out."

"What about up there, on the shelf?" exclaimed Tony, who had spotted a roll of colorful paper.

The man turned and looked.

"That's shelf paper," he said.

"Couldn't I have that?"

"I wanted to use it to line my shelves."

"Please!"

The man hesitated. He took down the roll and looked at it.

"Actually," he said, "the pattern was too peppy for me anyway."

"Great!" said Tony happily. "And how much is it?"

Good thing he had brought his pocket money!

"Free," said the man. "I'll give it to you. And I'll throw in some ribbon."

He took a card with a green ribbon out of the drawer.

"Thank you," Tony said, surprised. "If I ever need paper again, I'll be sure to come here for it!"

"Please don't," said the man. "I'd like to put the next roll of paper on my shelves!"

Wrapping a Coffin

"You found packing paper?" The little vampire beamed as Tony returned with the roll of paper and the ribbon.

"Uh-huh," Tony mumbled.

He didn't feel like explaining to Rudolph the difference between packing paper and shelf paper. He just handed him the roll and said, "Here!"

"What? Me?" squeaked the vampire.

"You're the one who wanted a wrapped coffin."

"But"—he looked at Anna for help—"I'm far too clumsy. I'm sure I'll tear the paper."

"You'll just have to make an effort," Tony said with a grin, and enjoyed the sudden feeling of superiority.

"We'll help you," Anna said. "We just have to wrap the paper around it, as if it were a bandage."

"Okay, okay," grumbled the vampire.

With a pained expression, he began to roll out the paper. His hat slipped over his face. He looked so funny that Anna and Tony had to laugh. The vampire furiously hurled the hat onto the grass.

"Go ahead, laugh," he whined. "Instead of helping me wrap it!"

"I am!" said Anna indignantly. "I'm holding it up for you, aren't I?"

"But Tony's just standing there laughing!"

"Without me, you wouldn't even have the paper," Tony replied calmly. How many times had the vampire stood idly by when Tony was struggling with something? For example, back when he was staying in Tony's basement and Tony's father wanted to get the boards out of the cellar behind which they had hidden his coffin. The vampire had nearly driven Tony to despair with his always being too tired, or his complete indifference to Tony needing help. Now Tony had the upper hand—but as true as that was, he wasn't going to take advantage of the situation.

"All right, I'll help," he offered. "Go stand over there!"

Obediently, the vampire went to the other side of the coffin and waited there for Tony to roll the paper to him, while Anna held up the coffin. The little vampire caught the roll and unwound it enough so he could pass it back to Tony under the coffin. Then Tony unwound it and rolled it over the top of the coffin to Rudolph. Soon they had the coffin well wrapped.

Anna wound the ribbon around the middle of the coffin and tied a big bow. "Doesn't it look great?"

"Like a birthday present," said Tony.

The little vampire sighed deeply. "Well, at least no one'll suspect it's a coffin!"

With a contented smile, he bent down, picked up his hat, and put it back on his head.

"Shall we go?" he asked.

"Not me," said Anna.

Tony turned to her in amazement. "Aren't you coming to the platform?"

She shook her head silently. Her eyes had gone large and were brimming with tears.

"Good luck, Tony," she said quietly. "See you soon!"

With that, she spread her cape and flew off.

"She didn't wish *me* good luck," the vampire whined. "And I might never come back."

Tony had to laugh. Rudolph was jealous!

"She left me to do everything now!" the vampire complained. "She could have at least carried the coffin to the train!"

"She probably did it to protect you," Tony replied.

"Whadda you mean?"

"So as not to draw attention to us. After all, she wasn't wearing a costume like you are."

"Oh right," the vampire remembered. "I almost forgot." Full of pride, he looked down at himself. "I'm not a vampire anymore. Now I'm—" He paused and then said smugly, "Rudy Sackville-Bagg the Beautiful!"

Tony struggled to suppress a laugh.

"We have to hurry," he said. "The train leaves in two minutes."

The vampire jumped. "Oh no!" he exclaimed, running to one end of the coffin. "Come on, Tony!"

Tony stood still.

"You could say 'please,'" he lectured the little vampire.

"All right, please!" said the vampire, gritting his teeth. "Now, will you come on?"

"All right," said Tony graciously, lifting the other end of the coffin.

We Like Birds, We're Related

As they crossed the station hall, the man in the kiosk was busy arranging bottles on a shelf and had his back to them. The woman at the ticket office was bent over a book writing something, and gave them only a cursory glance with no sign of surprise or alarm. She obviously didn't find the little vampire's appearance out of the ordinary. There was no one else about. Tony breathed a sigh of relief. He had imagined that their walk through the station hall was going to be like running the gauntlet, with them being watched suspiciously from all sides.

Even on the platform everything was fine. He had had no reason to worry. Apart from the ladies in their long green coats, who were pacing slowly up and down, paying no attention to them whatsoever, they were the only ones waiting for the train.

"They have great hats!" said the little vampire, pointing to the women.

"Don't make a spectacle of yourself," said Tony. "It'll draw their attention to us."

"But their hats are much nicer than mine," the vampire pouted. "Theirs have a tuft instead of a feather."

"A what?"

"A tuft. It looks like a brush."

Now Tony was curious, so he looked over. The hats were decorated with a thick, short tuft of hair.

"That's a chamois's beard," he explained. "It comes from a chamois, a kind of goat."

The vampire grimaced.

"Yuck! A goat!" he shrieked. "Vampires don't like goats!"

He tenderly stroked the feather on his hat. "But we like birds! We're related."

His outcry had apparently startled the two women. They had stopped and were looking over at Tony and Rudolph, worried.

Tony quickly moved in front of the little vampire and began to whistle the song "Yellow Bird."

Out of the corner of his eye, he saw the women exchange a look. Then they shook their heads in bewilderment and went back to their pacing.

At that moment the train arrived. It thundered and roared; its brakes screeched. The vampire stared at the long cars in fascination.

"A train, a real train!" he said ecstatically.

"If you spend too much time staring at it, it'll leave without you," Tony remarked sarcastically.

He had watched the two women get into the first car. The vampire's already pale face went paler.

"Oh no, that can't happen!" he shouted, grabbing the coffin in the middle and carrying it to the train.

Tony ran after him and held the train door open.

Finding Seats

"We did it!" exclaimed the vampire once they had jumped onto the third-to-last car and put the coffin near the door.

"Not yet!" replied Tony.

"Whadda you mean?"

"We can't stay here in the corridor."

Puzzled, the vampire asked, "Why not?"

"Because too many people pass by here. We have to find seats. I'll go see if I can find an empty compartment."

"What about me?" the vampire whimpered.

"You're waiting here," Tony said.

"And if someone comes?"

"Then you hide in the toilet." Tony pointed to the door

with the toilet sign. "Lock yourself in. I'll knock three times when I'm back."

"And my coffin?"

"Coffin? I don't see a coffin!" Tony grinned. "Oh, do you mean that long, beautifully wrapped surprise present?"

But the little vampire was in no mood for jokes. He said with dignity, "I will not leave my coffin unguarded. Especially not in a—"

"Train," he probably wanted to say, but then the train started with a jolt. The vampire took a few staggering steps and involuntarily sat down on his coffin. Surprised and speechless, he looked at Tony, who was struggling to keep a straight face.

But how was the little vampire supposed to know that he had to hold on when the train started? Tony realized. After all, he had never taken a train before.

"You'd better just sit there until I come back," he said. "I won't be long."

"Uh-huh." The vampire nodded. He was fine with not moving for the time being. He was clearly confused by the rumbling and rattling of the moving train. "But hurry up," he pleaded.

Tony pushed open the door that led to the compartments. He wanted to be like the heroes in the TV movies, very nonchalant and at ease. He pulled the corners of his mouth down, trying to look cool and collected as he walked down the hall with slow, swaying cowboy strides. After all, it was almost nine o'clock, and he couldn't allow himself to look like an anxious little schoolboy!

But there was no audience for Tony's cinematic performance. In the first compartment a woman sat by the window. Her head was back, and she had obviously fallen asleep. In the second one there was a man reading a newspaper, and Tony could only see his legs. The rest of the compartments were empty. Tony opted for the fourth one. If anyone were to board later, they would certainly sit in one of the empty ones, he thought.

"Did you find us some seats?" the vampire asked excitedly as Tony returned.

Tony gave a superior smile. "Come and see," he said.

Safe

With an anxious look at the swaying floor, the vampire stood up. "Is it far?"

"Only four compartments down," Tony told him.

Sighing, the vampire lifted one end of the coffin. Tony grabbed the other end. It seemed to him even heavier and bulkier than usual, as they carried it through the narrow corridor to their compartment. Once they were in, Tony quickly shut the door.

Now they were safe—for the time being. The vampire seemed to think so too. Breathing a sigh of relief, he fell back into the soft seat and stretched out.

"And your coffin?" cried Tony.

"What about my coffin?"

"We can't just leave it here between the seats!"

"Well, where else can we put it?"

"Up on the luggage rack."

Puzzled, the vampire looked around the compartment. "Luggage rack? What's that?"

"That thing up there," Tony explained impatiently. "That's a luggage rack."

"Oh, I see—"

The vampire took off his hat, stroked the feather lovingly, and placed it on the seat next to him. Then he calmly crossed his thin legs. "You're perfectly welcome to put it up there," he said. "That's fine."

Tony's jaw dropped in astonishment.

"M-me?" he cried. "Do you really think I can put this monstrous thing up there on my own?"

The vampire gave him a condescending look before rising majestically. "Yes, just as I thought," he said as he lifted the coffin and placed it seemingly effortlessly on the luggage rack. "You see, it's easy."

"But you usually claim you're so weak!" said Tony indignantly.

"That just depends on whether I've eaten something beforehand or not," the vampire said from up on the seat.

Tony shuddered. "S-so you've already eaten today?"

"Of course," said the vampire, licking his lips, remembering. "Or would you have preferred me to eat on the train . . . ?"

"No, no!" exclaimed Tony, horrified.

He noticed that he suddenly felt a bit strange. He got the impression that there was a menacing look in the vampire's red eyes, which were fixed on his neck. . . . But wasn't the vampire his friend? Tony gulped. "I—uh, brought something with me," he stuttered, pulling a small game box out from his inside jacket pocket. "Catch the Hat!"

"Catch the what?" the vampire asked in a grumbly voice.

"Catch the Hat," Tony replied anxiously. But to his relief, the vampire said, "Hats are nice!" while stroking his Tyrolean hat.

When Tony had put the game in his pocket at home,

he had felt a bit silly, thinking: imagine, playing a board game on a train with a vampire! But now he was glad that they had something to pass the time—so that the vampire didn't get any stupid ideas.

Rudolph looked at the box. "Does someone win?" he asked.

"Of course," Tony quickly assured him.

"Okay then, what are you waiting for?"

Vampire Hats

Tony sat down opposite the vampire by the window. He took the board and the pieces out of the box, placed them on the folding table between them, and pointed to the little hats. "What color do you want to be?"

The vampire croaked out a laugh. "Red, what else?"

A shiver ran down Tony's spine. But he didn't say anything. He just turned the board so the red area faced the little vampire and then handed him the four red hats.

He selected the yellow hats and put them down on the yellow area.

"How do you play?" grumbled the vampire.

"I'll show you," replied Tony. He then took one red and one yellow hat and put them on the board with three squares between them.

"You could catch me if you roll a four," he explained, "like this." He put the die down with the four facing up, took the red hat, advanced it four squares, and put it over the yellow hat. "Now the yellow one is caught!"

The vampire smiled happily. "And what do you do with the prisoners?" he asked.

"You try to bring them back to your section, or 'home,'" Tony replied, pointing to the red area in front of the vampire.

"And then what happens to them?" The vampire's eyes twinkled expectantly.

"Nothing," said Tony, puzzled by the question. "Whoever has the most hats in the end wins."

"That's it?" asked the vampire, disappointed. "Human games are not exactly exciting!"

"Whadda you mean?" asked Tony, astonished.

"We need to make up new rules," the little vampire said, pointing to a golden hat that was still in the box. "What's that one for?"

"I dunno," replied Tony.

The vampire picked up the hat and twisted it between his skinny fingers.

"I've got an idea," he said.

"What?" asked Tony.

"This golden hat," the vampire explained, "is going to be a vampire hat!"

"A v-vampire hat?" Tony looked puzzled.

"All the hats that are bitten by—er, caught—by this hat will then become vampire hats," the vampire said, giggling. "In the end, all the hats will be vampire hats. Doesn't that sound fun?"

"Well," Tony said evasively. He was not convinced by the vampire's idea. "We can try it out."

The vampire eagerly pushed his four red hats to him, so Tony now had eight hats. Then the vampire placed the golden hat in the middle of his red section.

"You can go first," he said cheerfully.

Tony rolled a six. He took a yellow hat and advanced it six squares.

Then the vampire rolled a two. "Hey, that's not fair," he

said indignantly, and wanted to roll the die again.

"It's my turn!" protested Tony, and reached for the die. Disgruntled, the vampire advanced his golden hat two squares.

Now Tony rolled the die and got a five.

With his index finger, the vampire counted how many fields separated the two hats.

"Three . . . ," he murmured. "I've almost got you!"

He rolled the die: six. "Darn!" he grumbled, and advanced his hat six squares.

Tony bit his lip so as not to laugh and rolled the die: three!

The vampire froze.

"I won!" cried Tony with poorly concealed triumph. The vampire's mouth began to twitch.

"Won?" he exclaimed in a loud voice. "It's a trick!"

"Not at all!" said Tony. "I just had better luck with the die than you."

"Luck! Luck!" hissed the vampire, giving Tony the evil eye. "Here's what I think of your stupid game."

He hit the board so hard that it flew up in the air and landed on the floor between the seats.

The hats were scattered across the seats and the floor. The die landed in front of the compartment door.

Tony's first thought was to jump up angrily. But then he told himself that the vampire was trying to get a rise out of him, and so he sat there quietly and looked out the window instead. It had become very dark outside, and he counted the lights flashing by.

As he had predicted, his apparent indifference confused the vampire. He slid nervously back and forth across the seat, looking at Tony. After a while, he asked, "Aren't you angry?"

"No," lied Tony. With a secret joy, he added, "I'm just thinking about whether I should go sit in another compartment."

"What?" yelled the vampire. "In another compartment? And what'll happen to me then?"

Tony had to smile. "All we do is argue when we're together, anyway, so I'm sure you'd much rather be alone."

"No!" cried the vampire. His lips trembled and his red eyes flickered. "I—I don't know how to behave on a train," he stammered.

"Clearly," Tony agreed.

"And besides, I—I'm completely helpless without you!"

Tony smiled, flattered. "If that's really true," he said cunningly, "maybe you should be a little more polite to me."

"I will," the vampire quickly promised.

"Good!" said Tony. "Then you can start by picking up the game."

Rudolph Tells a Story

After having picked up the game, the vampire asked with unusual courtesy, "Should we play again?"

"Really?" said Tony. "It wasn't that much fun last time."

"But if we play the way you wanted . . . ?"

"No. There's no point."

"Why not?"

"Because you always wanna win."

"Me?" the vampire said indignantly. "You started it! You're the one who said you win with the most hats."

"But who asked about winning?" retorted Tony.

"You did, of course!" said the vampire.

The vampire's audacity rendered Tony temporarily speechless. Then he said angrily, "You're just like your brother Gregory, who hates to lose."

But instead of being hurt by the comment, the vampire smiled, delighted. "You think so?"

Then he added, "I wish Gregory had heard that! He always tells me I'm strange, the white sheep of the family, so to speak."

"You?!" said Tony bitterly. "No, you're not!"

"Yes, yes, that's what he says!" The little vampire leaned back in his seat and crossed his legs.

"One night, Gregory and I had been commissioned by the family council to teach Ravenhood a lesson," he told him. "At midnight we were to go to his house and ring the bell. Brr!" He shivered, remembering it.

Tony could well imagine how the vampire must have felt, because he too shivered every time he thought of the cemetery caretaker, who was obsessed with his ambition to destroy the vampires and their graves, and therefore always carried sharpened wooden stakes and a hammer with him when he roamed around the cemetery.

"And?" asked Tony.

"And I was supposed to lure him out of his house by

shouting, 'Mr. Ravenhood, your woodshed's on fire!' Then Gregory was supposed to bite him. Just a small bite, a warning. And then I was supposed to write: 'Vampire graves here, Ravenhood, don't come near!' on the door with red paint."

Tony shuddered at the idea. "So what happened?" he begged.

"Well . . ." The vampire visibly enjoyed Tony's full attention. "I rang the bell. Nothing happened. Gregory stirred in the bushes next to me. I went weak in the knees. I rang the bell again. The shrill sound shook the silence that surrounded us. . . ."

"Hey, get on with it. The suspense is killing me!" insisted Tony.

"And suddenly, footsteps! Light, shuffling footsteps approached the door. Then someone coughed. I felt sick. . . ."

"Me too," Tony mumbled.

"Then I heard Ravenhood's hoarse voice. 'What is it?' he asked. A wave of garlic fumes came out of the cracks in the door and wafted over me. Everything went black for a second. I nearly passed out. I wanted to speak, but I couldn't. Nothing came out. Then Gregory shouted, 'Mr. Ravenhood, your woodshed's on fire!' The door opened, but I wasn't face-to-face with Ravenhood—"

"You weren't?"

"No, it was some creature with eyes like glowing coals. It let out a screech that chilled me to the bone, then leapt . . . and landed on my shoulder!"

Tony stared open-mouthed at the vampire. "On your shoulder? Was it that small?"

The vampire lowered his head.

"It was a cat," he said, ashamed.

"A cat?" said Tony, surprised.

"Yes. Ravenhood's cat. He had been careful enough to stand in the shadow of the door, holding the cat in his arms, so I could only see the cat's shining eyes. When he realized who was standing at his door, he threw the cat at me." The vampire faltered. There were beads of sweat on his pale forehead. "I was so scared that I ran away without looking back. 'Just wait till I catch you, you rascal!' I heard Ravenhood shout after me, but I ran faster than I had ever run before."

"How do you know it was a cat?" asked Tony.

"Gregory told me later. He watched the whole thing from the bushes without Ravenhood seeing him. And ever since then I have been called the white sheep of the family, because I got scared by a cat." He wore such a sad expression that Tony had to laugh.

"I'd have been scared too," he said, trying to comfort the vampire. "I think it was incredibly brave of you to have even rung Ravenhood's doorbell."

"Really?" The vampire found a smile again.

"Really! And everyone gets scared sometimes."

"Even a vampire," said the little vampire with a sigh.

Unwelcome Surprise

The vampire picked up his hat and put it back on. "You're a real friend," he said warmly. "I can tell from the wonderful things you've given me." He gazed lovingly at the lederhosen and jacket. "You did give them to me, didn't you?"

"You mean as a present?" Tony had to laugh. "I'd love to! But I don't think my mom and grandma would be happy about—" He stopped and looked at the compartment door. "Did you hear something?"

"No," said the vampire. "Just the terrible train clattering!"

"Someone's coming!" whispered Tony.

The vampire froze. "In here?"

"Maybe it's the conductor?" Suddenly Tony remembered

what he had been meaning to ask the vampire. "Do you have your ID with you?"

"Of course! It's in the coffin!" said the vampire proudly.

"In the coffin?" cried Tony.

The vampire looked puzzled. "That's the safest place for it."

"Oh no!" groaned Tony, and held his head. Why hadn't he asked earlier? "What if the conductor comes and wants to see your ID?"

"Ah—" Slowly the vampire seemed to understand. "You mean, because we wrapped the coffin . . ."

"Exactly! Then we'll have to unwrap it, and the conductor will see that it's not a present at all!"

The vampire's eyes went wide with fear. "Really?" His lips trembled. "So, whadda we do now?"

"I don't know," said Tony. Just then the compartment door opened, and a seemingly friendly lady looked in at them.

"Is there still space in here with you?" she asked.

Poyson—With a Y

Tony and the little vampire looked at each other in alarm.

"Well, uh—" Tony began. Somehow, he had to stop her from sitting in their compartment—but how? If he was too rude, there was the risk that she would complain to the conductor. "You know . . ."

The lady had apparently interpreted Tony's hesitation to mean the opposite and said, "That's very kind of you!" and came in.

Tony's heart skipped a beat. "B-but," he stuttered, looking at the little vampire for help. But the little vampire just watched, scowling, as the lady brought in a suitcase, a basket, and a plastic bag and stowed them on the luggage rack. Then she closed the compartment door and sat down on the seat next to the door, not far from Tony. She didn't seem to notice how unwelcome she was, because she said cheerfully, "Thank goodness, a nonsmoking compartment! I'm sure I'll be much more comfortable in here with you two. You know, I was just in a compartment with two gentlemen, very nice gentlemen, but their clothes smelled strongly of cigarette smoke. And since I can't stand that smell, I preferred to move."

She laughed and sniffed the air.

"But it smells funny in here too," she said. "Must be the old upholstery! By the way, my name is Mrs. Poyson, with a *y*. What are yours?"

"Ours?"

"Yes, yours." She turned to Tony and looked at him with squinting eyes.

"I can't really see you," she said suddenly. "Everything is so blurry." She touched her eyes.

"My glasses!" she exclaimed. "I didn't put my glasses on!" She began to search desperately through her purse.

Tony bit his lip, because he could see her glasses. They

were sticking slightly out of the breast pocket of her jacket.

The vampire had also noticed them and drew Tony's attention to them with a nod of the head.

"Where are they?" she mumbled to herself. "Did I leave them at my daughter's house? Yes, that must be it! I must have left them there!"

Tony giggled furtively. He felt a little guilty because he wasn't telling her where her glasses were. On the other hand, it was much safer for him and the little vampire to sit in a compartment with someone who couldn't see properly. Knowing that, Tony now dared to look at her more closely. How old could she be? Fifty, sixty? She was definitely younger than his grandmother, and *she* was already over sixty. In any case, she didn't look like a grandma, he thought. She wore a pantsuit, a colorful scarf, a pearl necklace, and large earrings. Her very blond hair was probably dyed, he decided.

It's No Joke

Giving up, the lady shut her purse and sighed. "Luckily, I've got a spare pair at home!"

Tony and the little vampire exchanged conspiratorial smiles. But their good cheer did not last long.

"What was your name?" the lady asked.

"My name?" Tony said, looking at the vampire for help. But he just shrugged helplessly.

"Well, me—I'm Tony Noodleman," he finally said hesitantly. "And this—that's my brother, Rudolph Sackville-Bagg."

"Brothers? Oh, how nice! But why do you have two different surnames?"

"Two different surnames, oh yes . . ." He hadn't

considered that. But he quickly came up with a reason. "Our mother married twice, you see. My brother comes from her first marriage. He's also *much* older."

Tony had put so much emphasis on the "much" that she asked with amusement, "*So* much? How old is he then?"

That shocked Tony. What was he going to say?

"Fourteen," answered the vampire in his place.

"Fourteen?" she repeated, laughing. "Then you are both still minors. Tony and—"

"Rudolph," growled the vampire.

"Tony and Rudolph! And I thought you were both grown-ups! Me with my bad eyes! Are you even allowed to be out so late at night on your own? Won't your mother worry?"

"No, she won't," answered the vampire.

"We're going to our aunt's house—in the country," Tony quickly added.

"Oh, and where?"

"To Little Ol' Molting."

"To Little Ol' Molting?" she exclaimed in surprise. "Then we're going to the same place!"

"Oh!" said Tony, startled. "Are you also going to Little Ol' Molting?"

"No." She laughed. "But I have to get off at Big Ol' Molting too. I live in Millton, a nearby town."

"Great," Tony whispered to the vampire.

"What's your aunt's name?"

"What is our a-aunt's n-name?" Tony flinched. He had, of course, long forgotten the name of the family they were going to stay with. He only remembered the address, 13 Old Town Road. But of course he wasn't going to tell her that!

"I don't remember her last name," he said. "We always call her Auntie Mary." He figured there were probably several women named Mary in Little Ol' Molting, so the lady wouldn't realize he was making it up.

"Mary, Mary..." She was thinking. "Mary Pepperbrink?"

Tony bit his tongue so as not to laugh and shook his head. "No."

"Mary Rosenbloom?"

"No."

"Oh well," she said, "I don't really know Little Ol' Molting that well. It's about twenty miles from Millton."

Luckily! Tony smiled at the vampire.

"So your aunt will pick you up at the station, then?"

"Uh . . . why?"

"Because it's about a mile to Little Ol' Molting."

"Mmmm, yes," Tony answered, looking over at the little vampire for help, but he just sat there, nervously cracking his knuckles.

"If not, we'll be happy to take you to Little Ol' Molting. My husband will be waiting for me at the station with his car."

"No, no, that won't be necessary, but thank you very much," said Tony hastily. "Of course our aunt will be picking us up! Besides, I'm sure our present won't fit in your car." He pointed up to the wrapped coffin.

She blinked. "That's pretty big!"

"There's a lot in it too," Tony explained. "All the things

that are hard to find in the countryside. Shirts, trousers, towels, toothbrushes, socks, aftershave—" He broke off because he couldn't think of anything else.

Grinning, the vampire added, "And blood! Blood in bottles, blood in jars, blood in cans . . ."

"Excuse me?" said the lady, surprised. "Blood?"

"My brother's just kidding," Tony quickly explained to reassure the lady.

"You shouldn't joke about things like that!" she lectured him. "Blood is something very precious. Our life source! But of course, you children are too young to understand that yet. Or do you know why our body needs blood?"

"Do I know why our body needs blood . . ." Tony paused. He stared seriously at the vampire. "No!"

"Well, I'll tell you. Blood supplies our body with nutrients and oxygen. I know that because I used to be a blood donor."

"Blood donor?" Suddenly the vampire's eyes sparkled,

and his teeth clicked together. "Was your blood that good?"

She laughed smugly. "Yes! And it still is!"

"But you are now no longer a donor, then?" the vampire asked in a rough, throaty voice.

"No."

"Then you must be full of blood!"

"Yes." She laughed again.

Fortunately, she didn't seem to have noticed that the vampire had bared his horrible fangs and was now rising from his seat slowly, inch by inch, with an ecstatic look on his face.

For a second, Tony was paralyzed with fright. Then he jumped up, threw himself at the vampire, and pushed him back into his seat.

"Rudolph!" he shouted, shaking him.

"What is it?" the lady asked worriedly. "Is your brother feeling queasy with all this talk of blood? Is he squeamish?"

"Yes, yes," Tony quickly agreed. "Very squeamish. It's his stomach. He probably hasn't had enough to eat."

"Oh, your brother's hungry!" she said. "If that's all it is, then . . ." She got up and took her basket down from the luggage rack.

"I've brought plenty to eat!"

Picnic for Three

The lady placed a white cloth on the seat between herself and Tony and began to lay out the contents of her basket: two sausage rolls, two cheese sandwiches, three hard-boiled eggs, two apples, two tomatoes, a bar of peppermint chocolate, and a thermos.

Everything looked so delicious that Tony's mouth was watering. At home at dinner, he had hardly been able to swallow, he was so nervous. All he had managed was some juice and a few crackers. Now his stomach was rumbling.

"Dig in!" she encouraged him.

"Thank you," said Tony, and took a cheese sandwich.

"What about your brother? What would he like?"

"Uh . . . a sausage roll!"

The vampire raised his hands in protest, but Tony

handed him a sausage roll, insistent. "Take it!" he hissed. "You don't have to really eat it!"

The vampire looked at the roll in his hand with the sausage sticking out, disgusted. "And what am I supposed to do with this?" he asked.

Tony cast a worried glance over to the lady before answering. But she was busy pouring coffee from the thermos into a cup. She wasn't paying any attention to them.

"You just give it back to me," he explained in a whisper.

"Oh, okay!" The vampire sighed with relief.

The lady took a sip of coffee and asked, "How is it?"

"Good!" the vampire replied. He secretly gave the roll back to Tony, who ate it happily.

"I'm glad! I guess your mother didn't pack you anything to eat on the way?"

"No," said Tony with his mouth full.

She shook her head in disbelief. "Children need to be taken care of! Well, now you've got me," she added, laughing. "You may call me Auntie Greta. But don't eat it all!"

"We won't," said Tony, taking an apple. He had almost choked when she'd said "Auntie Greta."

"And what about you, Rudolph? Have you had enough?" She squinted questioningly in the little vampire's direction.

"Not quite," replied the vampire in a croaky voice.

"He'd like a tomato," Tony said quickly.

"Just a tomato?" She took a paper plate out of her basket. "Even though he's really hungry? No, I'll put together a really nice plate for him!"

She put a hard-boiled egg, an apple, a tomato, two squares of chocolate, and the second sausage roll on the plate, then handed it to Tony. "Here! It will do your brother good!"

Tony had to bite his tongue not to laugh. The plate shook in his hand as he passed it to the little vampire.

"Thank you, Auntie Greta," groaned the vampire. He put the plate down on the small table next to the hat game and pretended to eat, while secretly handing the chocolate to Tony.

"Do you often travel alone by train?" the lady asked.

"Us? No!" said Tony.

"Not even to your aunt's?"

"No, we always fly," said the vampire with a growly laugh.

"Your brother's quite a kidder!" said the lady, slightly annoyed.

"Idiot!" hissed Tony at the vampire. Turning to the lady, he said, "Don't mind him. He's going through a difficult stage, as our mother calls it."

She nodded in understanding. "Oh, that's why!"

Fortunately, she couldn't see how angry the vampire was at being insulted.

"But it won't last," she said. "In a year at the most, your brother will turn into a nice young man."

They're Just Stories

"**J**ust like the young man in the book I'm reading, this lawyer, what was his name?"

The lady took a book out of her purse and leafed through it, only to slam it shut again immediately afterward. "Oh, I can't read without glasses!"

The book had aroused Tony's curiosity. He had recognized a bat on the back cover! He twisted his head, trying to read the title.

"The book is supposed to be very exciting," the lady continued. "My daughter passed it on to me after she'd read it in one night. It's the story of a young man, an Englishman, who is sent on a business trip to the Carpathians. He is supposed to visit a strange count in his castle—"

"Count Dracula?" exclaimed Tony breathlessly.

The vampire was also listening.

Surprised, the lady asked, "Do you know the book?"

"A little," Tony said bashfully. She didn't need to know that it was his favorite book!

"Do you also like to read scary books?" Her voice was full of enthusiasm. "My daughter and I are obsessed with scary stories. But they have to be really scary so that chills run down our spines. We like to read them after dark, when the wind is howling around the house and things are creaking and whispering eerily everywhere. . . ." She let out a deep sigh. "We're especially fond of vampire stories. They're so"—she searched for the right word—"so romantic!"

The little vampire gave a hollow laugh. Being a vampire was anything but romantic! "They're just stories," he growled.

"Thank goodness!" she laughed. "That's what's so great about them. You can read the most horrible things, and at the same time you know it's all just fantasy!"

"Fantasy?" said the vampire hoarsely.

"There aren't really such things as spirits, ghosts, or vampires—"

"Oh, really?" the vampire exclaimed.

The lady laughed. "Do you really believe that there are dead people who come out of their graves at night to suck people's blood? I don't!"

The vampire let out a soft, menacing growl. Tony gestured, imploring him not to get angry and to just stay calm.

The lady didn't seem to notice. She went on cheerfully, "Have you ever met a vampire? A deadly pale, half-rotten corpse with pointed fangs?"

She broke off because the compartment door had opened. A man in uniform entered and said, "Tickets, please!"

The Conductor

An icy fright ran through Tony. With trembling fingers, he reached into his jacket pocket, where he had put the two tickets he had bought on Monday after school. Luckily, there had been enough money in his piggy bank.

"Here," he mumbled, handing them to the conductor, who took them with a nod. *Hopefully everything is all right,* Tony thought anxiously.

"So, you're going to Big Ol' Molting?" Through his glasses, he looked first at Tony and then at the little vampire. The vampire quickly pulled his hat so far into his forehead that not much of his face was showing.

"Yes—uh, I mean, no," Tony stuttered. "Actually, we want to go to Little Ol' Molting."

"To Little Ol' Molting," said the conductor.

His voice sounded so strange that Tony wondered if it was just a normal grown-up tone—or if they had aroused suspicion. To his great relief, the lady, who was still searching through her purse, said, "They're going to visit their aunt."

"You know them?" the conductor asked.

"That's Auntie Greta!" the vampire said in a raspy voice.

The conductor looked surprised. "Oh, so you're traveling together!"

"Yes, yes," said the lady absentmindedly as she continued to rummage through her purse.

"Well, if that's the case," said the conductor, "I won't worry that there are two underaged boys traveling alone this late at night!"

At that moment, the lady gave a sigh of relief. "Finally, I found it!" she exclaimed, handing her ticket to the conductor. He took a quick look at it and gave it back to her.

Embarrassed, she said, "Sorry it took so long. But I forgot my glasses at my daughter's house."

"Your glasses?" said the conductor in surprise. "But

they're in your jacket pocket!" With that, he turned toward the door. "We'll be in Big Ol' Molting in ten minutes!" he said. Then he closed the compartment door behind him and walked away to the left, in the direction of travel.

You're Wrong About Us

"**M**y glasses? In my jacket pocket?" said the lady incredulously. "Is that true?"

Tony didn't answer. He only knew that he and the little vampire had to disappear before she found them and put them on!

She searched the side pockets of her jacket. But they weren't there. But it wouldn't be long before she had the idea to look in the breast pocket. . . .

"We have to go!" he hissed at the vampire.

"Go?" The vampire looked unhappily between the door and the window. "Where?"

"Outside, into the corridor. Anywhere, but we have to get away from here!"

"And my coffin?"

"We'll take it with us, of course."

A surprised cry from the lady interrupted their excited whispers. "Here they are!" she exclaimed. Shaking her head, she pulled her glasses out of her breast pocket. "And I actually thought I'd left them at my daughter's!" She took a silk scarf from her purse, breathed on the glasses, and began to clean them. She looked at Tony with a squint and said sternly and reproachfully, "And you just let me sit here like this, even though you knew exactly where my glasses were. Instead of helping me, you made fun of me!"

"Us? No, not at all!" Tony had just put the hat game back in his inside pocket.

"Come on!" He nudged the vampire. "She's about to finish cleaning her glasses!"

He and the vampire both stood up.

"Yes, yes," said the lady. "You were mocking me! That silly old lady, you were thinking, let's let her frantically look for her glasses, she can't see anything anyway."

"No," Tony objected as he and the vampire lifted the heavy coffin out of the luggage rack. "We only just noticed your glasses." He didn't think she believed him, but at least she was distracted and was only thinking about cleaning her glasses for the time being and not putting them on. If he managed to distract her until they had taken the coffin out of the compartment, they were saved. . . .

It seemed to be working, as she continued to clean her glasses.

"Just noticed, ha!" She laughed angrily. "You knew all along where my glasses were!"

Meanwhile, Tony had opened the compartment door. "You're wrong about us," he said, still trying to distract her.

"Now!" He nodded to the vampire, and together they lifted the coffin they had rested on the vampire's row of seats for a moment.

"Oh really, I'm wrong about you?" Her voice had taken on an irritated tone. "We'll see about that, as soon as I have my glasses on!"

Tony was already out in the corridor with the front part of the coffin. The little vampire, on the other hand, who was carrying the rear, was still in the compartment.

With an anxious feeling of dread, Tony turned around and saw how the lady stared at the little vampire through her glasses, stunned. She opened her mouth to scream— but only a hoarse whisper came out. "A vampire, a real vampire . . . !"

Then she fainted motionless against the seat.

"Is she dead?" the vampire asked.

"No, she just fainted," replied Tony, who had become very weak in the knees. He had often seen people faint on TV, but it was quite something else in real life.

"Come on!" he whispered to the vampire, who looked ecstatically at the lady's white neck, which was bare where the scarf had slipped down. "Or do you want to wait until she wakes up and calls the conductor?"

"I'm coming," said the vampire.

Nevertheless, he stayed rooted to the spot, casting greedy glances at the lady's neck.

Tony was getting more and more restless. A passenger or the conductor could come by at any moment. . . .

"If you stand there one minute longer," he said angrily, "you'll be finding your way to Little Ol' Molting without me!"

This threat seemed to work. The vampire suddenly looked guilty and embarrassed. "I'm coming," he said.

Free and Clear

Carefully, they carried the coffin through the door and even managed not to bump into anything. Once in the corridor, Tony, who was also carrying his tote bag, set down the front of the coffin with a groan and rubbed his aching fingers.

"I'd love to know if you'd struggle for me like this," he said, gritting his teeth.

"I—I'll carry the coffin on my own," the vampire said quickly. "You just tell me where to go!"

As always, when Tony was justifiably complaining about him, the little vampire distracted him. But they were in too much of a hurry to discuss it now, so Tony simply said, "Turn right."

Since the conductor had gone to the left, it seemed

best if they went in the opposite direction toward the last car and got off there.

On shaky legs, with his eyes fixed on the swaying ground, the vampire carried his coffin down the corridor. Beads of sweat formed on his forehead and his teeth chattered loudly. Once through the door that Tony held open for him, he dropped the coffin with a thump and sat down on it, exhausted.

"Hey, we have to keep going!" exclaimed Tony with urgency.

"I don't feel well," moaned the vampire.

"Do you want the conductor to find us?"

"No. But my head is spinning." The vampire looked so miserable that Tony actually felt sorry for him. "Can't I just sit here for a while?"

"Hmm," said Tony, unsure. They would definitely be safer in the last car. But on the other hand, it couldn't be that much longer to Big Ol' Molting, because the train was already slowing down, and he could see the lit windows of houses on both sides of the train.

"All right," he said. "But be discreet!"

This warning was probably unnecessary, Tony thought, because the little vampire would certainly not do anything stupid. But it made Tony feel good to remind him, once again, that he was dependent on Tony, and that Tony could tell the vampire how to behave. The vampire just gave him a dirty look but said nothing.

"I hope you'll feel better when we're in Big Ol' Molting," said Tony. "Because I can't carry the coffin on my own."

"Of course I will," growled the vampire. "I'll be fine once this terrible rattling and rumbling stops!" And, in fact, the vampire looked much better once the train entered the station. Without any prompting from Tony, the little vampire stood up and pushed his coffin to the door.

Tony had, in the meantime, peered out the window in the door. He was relieved to find that their car was stopping at the back of the platform, well away from the station building, where an elderly gentleman with a bouquet of flowers was pacing up and down.

Opposite where they were was a bicycle stand, and just

beyond it was a narrow path lined with dense bushes. They could get there quickly and safely—as long as the vampire cooperated and didn't leave Tony in the lurch!

Worried, Tony turned to look at him. But his fear of seeing the little vampire just sitting on the coffin was unfounded. The vampire had already lifted his coffin end and was just waiting for Tony to lift the front.

They made their way off the train, then Tony paused.

"Everything all right?" Rudolph asked in a hoarse voice.

Tony nodded. "There's a little overgrown path just ahead of us. We should be safe over there."

When they had reached the bushes, Tony looked back again. He saw the lady from their compartment slowly coming down the steps off the train, supported by the gentleman with the bouquet of flowers. And farther along, he saw two women looking around the station. They wore long green coats, Tyrolean hats, and hiking boots.

"Oh dear, them again!" he moaned. "We'd better go!"

"Them, who?" the vampire asked.

"The women with the nice hats," Tony replied bluntly. Now was really not the time to talk about them, he thought. It was much more important to find out where the path led and how to get to Little Ol' Molting.

At the start of the path, Tony stopped. "We should put the coffin down here and look around first." He had to speak very loudly, because at that moment the train was pulling out.

"What! And leave my coffin unguarded?" the vampire said indignantly. "Never! I'd rather sit on it until you come back."

That suited Tony perfectly, because he could move freely on his own. Grinning, he said, "But be—"

"—discreet, I know!" the vampire said angrily. "Don't worry, sir!"

Getting to Little Ol' Molting

A s Tony walked down the path, he saw that it led to the road, just as he had suspected. What surprised him was that there was no fence, no barrier, not even trampled wire mesh.

The advantages of small-town stations, he thought happily. He'd been afraid that they would have to lift the coffin over a high wall or a barbed-wire fence or, even worse, go through the station.

The road lay deserted in the glow of the lamps. Two cars were parked in front of the station building, a black sedan and a light blue station wagon. The road seemed to end at the station, because everything behind the fore-court was dark.

At the other end of the road, Tony saw a large building.

NEST-EGG INN was written on the neon sign. The inn was on a wide road, probably the main road. There were two other signs.

One pointed to the left and read OLD CAIRN, 8 MILES, and just below it, in a smaller font: LITTLE OL' MOLTING, 1 MILE. And the second sign pointed to the right and read MILLTON, 15 MILES.

Tony sighed with relief: now at least he knew in which direction they had to go. And compared to the train ride, the last mile to Little Ol' Molting would be a cakewalk! A bit exhausting maybe, with the heavy coffin—but not half as nerve-racking! Tony heard the cars pulling off from in front of the station. He hid behind a large fir tree, so he could watch the road without being seen.

The black sedan drove past him first. The elderly gentle-man was driving. He recognized Mrs. Poyson next to him, leaning her head back. The car drove to the main road and turned right. Then came the light blue station wagon. It was driven by a woman. In the back seat were the two women with the

Tyrolean hats. Tony watched them turn left toward Old Cairn.

He waited for a bit longer and listened. A muffled babble of voices floated over to him from the inn. A car honked in the distance. On the other side of the tracks a dog barked. *Small-town nightlife!* thought Tony. Fortunately, no one knew a vampire had just come to town. And if everything went well, no one would ever know! Tony turned around and walked back down the path. The little vampire was waiting for him impatiently.

"I was worried you weren't coming back," he said.

Tony smiled. "And what would you have done without me? Gone in search of the town cemetery?"

The vampire shot him an angry look. "Just help me with the coffin," he growled. He squinted at Tony's neck and added threateningly, "Or do ya wanna wait till I get hungry?"

"Till you're hungry?" responded Tony, frightened. "Uh, Little Ol' Molting is really close. It's only a mile away. We can do that in no time."

"Do you know the way?"

"Yes."

"All right, let's go!"

They lifted the coffin and carried it to the end of the road. There Tony looked left and right, then nodded to the vampire. "Come on," he whispered. The door of the inn was open as they passed by. Loud music poured out, but no one was around. In the shadow of a car parked in front of the inn, Tony stopped.

"What is it?" the vampire hissed. "Don't you know which way to go?"

"Yes. I'm just thinking about which side of the road is safer."

The vampire looked across the street. "That one over there, of course! There aren't any houses. And we can hide in the bushes if a car comes."

"But it is very tedious to walk through tall grass," said Tony. He would have preferred to stay on this side and walk on the footpath. After all, they still had a ways to go, and his hands were already hurting.

But the vampire said firmly, "It's safer over there!"

"If you say so," said Tony.

They crossed the road and continued toward Little Ol' Molting.

After a while, Tony said, "I have to go."

"Go?" the vampire asked. "Go where?"

Tony cleared his throat. "I—uh—have to *go*."

A car was approaching. They quickly put down the coffin and ducked behind a bush.

"Don't you ever have to?" asked Tony.

"Ever have to what?"

"Well, uh—pee."

"Oh!" Finally the vampire had understood him. "That's what you mean! No, the last time I did was about a hundred years ago."

"Really?" wondered Tony. "Is that true of all vampires?"

The vampire looked at him and grinned. "Were you wondering if Anna needed to?"

"What made you think of Anna?" asked Tony. He noticed he was blushing, so he quickly said, "I'll just go!" and disappeared behind a tree.

"Hurry up!"

Soon they continued on their way. Tony's hands were burning, and his arms and shoulders felt like lead.

"You okay?" asked the vampire.

"Hmm," Tony said in a strained voice.

In the distance he saw the Little Ol' Molting town sign. He would be able to make it there!

Abandoned

Behind the town sign the road forked. Tony read the street signs: CAIRN ROAD was straight ahead. OLD TOWN ROAD was to the right.

"That's it!" he exclaimed excitedly.

"What?" the vampire asked suspiciously.

"The street we're looking for. Old Town Road. That's where we're going!"

The idea that they had actually reached their destination gave Tony new strength. He walked so fast that Rudolph could hardly keep up.

"There's the farm, up ahead!" Tony felt his heart beat faster. "See it? The big barn with the stable next to a white house."

"How do you know it's the right house?"

"Because I've been here before."

"And you're really sure?"

"Yes."

"Then I don't really need you anymore," the vampire explained.

Surprised, Tony stopped. "Whadda you mean?"

"I mean, I can manage the last stretch on my own."

"And what about me?"

"You can go home," the vampire said, indifferent.

Tony was speechless for a few seconds. Then he yelled, "Alone?"

"Why not?" said the vampire, astonished. "You'll be much safer on the train without me."

"But there isn't another train!"

"There isn't?"

"No! I asked earlier."

The vampire looked at Tony, surprised. "How were you planning to get home?"

"With you! I packed your second cape, which I still had from Anna."

"You have the cape with you? That's wonderful!" The vampire laughed hoarsely. "Then you don't need the train at all. You can just fly home!"

"Hey, you're being pretty selfish!" said Tony angrily. "I brought you out here, carried your heavy coffin—"

Suddenly he realized that they were still carrying the coffin. He dropped it heavily into the grass.

"Hey!" cried the vampire.

"—and now you don't want to be bothered to fly back with me!"

"You don't understand," said the vampire, slightly embarrassed. "I need to—" He paused and then finished, "Settle in."

"There you go again, thinking only of yourself!" said Tony bitterly.

"Vampires have to! Besides, flying alone's not so bad," he added. "After all, I do it every night, even though I'm afraid of the dark."

"And how am I supposed to find the way?"

"Just follow the tracks."

"What if someone sees me?"

The vampire waved his hand. "Everyone's asleep at this time of night. No one will see you."

"And what if I run into Aunt Dorothee?"

"She'll think you're a vampire and leave you alone."

Just then, a loud "baaaa" reached them from the barn. A hungry smile appeared on the vampire's pale face, and his fangs flashed in the moonlight.

"Did you hear that?" he whispered. "A sheep! A real live sheep. Full of blood!"

He grabbed his coffin and turned to go. "See you tomorrow!" he said, and disappeared between the trees.

Tony watched him leave. How could he have been so stupid to think that the vampire would accompany him back home? After all, it wasn't the first time the vampire had let him down. He was terrified at the thought of the long, lonely flight back. But there was no other solution. He had to do it! He took the vampire cape out of his bag and pulled it on. Then he spread his arms and flew unsteadily away—like a moth that had been burned by a bulb.

A Misjudgment

"**T**ony, wake up!"

Tony opened his eyes. Confused, he wondered where the sudden light was coming from. Wasn't he still flying through the night sky?

"Tony, hurry up!" It was his mother's voice. "It's time for breakfast."

"Breakfast?" mumbled Tony. But he had to fly home, follow the tracks. . . . Tony's bedroom door opened and his mother came in.

"Tony!" she said reproachfully. "We want to leave soon, and you're still in bed!"

Tony blinked. Then he was already home!

"We've finished breakfast, the suitcases are in the car—we're just waiting for you."

"All right, I'm coming." Tony sat up with difficulty. Everything hurt, and especially his shoulders and arms. They felt as though he had lifted weights for hours. He moaned softly.

"A night in front of the TV is pretty exhausting, isn't it?" said his mother.

"Why do you say that?"

"We didn't get back until two, but we're not half as tired as you are."

"What time is it?"

"Nine thirty."

"Nine thirty . . . ," Tony repeated slowly, scratching his head.

"Tell me honestly, how late did you stay up watching TV last night?"

"I didn't watch TV," Tony wanted to say, truthfully. But then he would have had to come up with another explanation for his sleeping late, and he was way too tired for that.

"Until eleven," he said.

"That late!" exclaimed his mother indignantly. "We explicitly said not past ten!"

"Are you coming to breakfast?" his father called from the kitchen.

"Tony watched TV until eleven!" his mother called back. "What do you think of that?"

"It—it was a really interesting show," said Tony.

"Really? What was it?"

That shook Tony. He had no idea what had been on TV last night.

"I forgot," he mumbled.

"Are you coming?" insisted Tony's father.

"I'll look it up," his mother said. "What channel?"

"Uh—two."

Tony's mother left. *I hope there wasn't a scary movie on last night!* he thought. Otherwise, his parents would be upset with him. He got up and got dressed. He then remembered the vampire cape he had stuffed under the mattress last night. He had to bring it with him to Little

Ol' Molting, but how? His suitcase was already packed in the car. He couldn't put it on. Perplexed, he looked around the room. His eyes fell on his bookbag next to his desk— and that gave him an idea.

"Hey, Mom?" he called. "Can I take my bookbag with me? I want to study for school."

"While you're on vacation?"

"Yes. I want to be better prepared for junior high."

"Of course you can!" she answered, but she sounded a bit suspicious, Tony thought. No wonder: this was the first time he had ever asked if he could take schoolwork on vacation. And she was right to be suspicious. The last thing he wanted to do during vacation was study!

He quickly folded the cape and had just managed to hide it under the schoolbooks and notebooks in his bookbag when his mother came into the room again. She looked suspiciously at the bag.

"And there really are schoolbooks in there?"

Tony had to suppress a smile. "Of course!"

"May I see?"

"Why?"

"Because I suspect that you're trying to smuggle your vampire books to Little Ol' Molting in your bookbag!"

"Mom!" protested Tony.

"But I do. And we definitely don't want that."

Tony considered the situation for a second. If she really wanted to look in his bookbag, there was nothing he could do. But maybe he would luck out and she wouldn't notice the cape!

With an uneasy feeling, he held the bookbag out to her.

She pulled out a few books and notebooks, read the covers, then shook her head in disbelief.

"All schoolbooks," she said to herself. "I misjudged you."

Tony grinned, content.

"But boy, does it smell!" she added, puzzled. "Really musty!"

Tony bit his lip so as not to laugh. "You think so?" He quickly snapped the locks on his bag.

"By the way," said his mother, "I must say, I am very surprised about your taste in TV shows."

"Why?"

"Saturday, eight p.m.: opera highlights, the ten o'clock nightly news, followed by folk music, until eleven," she read from the printout she had in her hand.

Tony blushed.

"I just felt like listening to some music," he said sheepishly.

"Opera followed by folk music? That's a change from your usual interests!"

"Well—" Tony cleared his throat. "Dad keeps saying you have to try everything once."

"Right. And now I'm *saying*, the eggs will get cold if you don't come right away." That was his father's voice from the kitchen.

"We're on our way," his mother replied. She went out first, with Tony right behind her, happy to have survived her probing questions.

Country Air Makes You Tired

Tony tried to read a comic book on the drive to Little Ol' Molting, but soon the words started to swim before his eyes.

"Tony is about to fall asleep again!" remarked his mother, who was driving and watching him in the rear-view mirror.

"It's the country air," said his father, who was looking at the map of Little Ol' Molting and the surrounding area. Tony stifled a laugh. They had barely been on the road a quarter of an hour, and the "country air" was putting him to sleep! On the other hand, he might need to use that excuse over the next few days.

"Yes, exactly, country air does make you tired," he said with a big yawn, as if to prove his point.

"It's probably more likely the opera highlights and folk music," his mother replied mockingly.

Tony chose not to answer. He read a few more pages of his comic. Then his eyes closed and he fell asleep.

It was night. Tony sat on the branch of a large oak tree resting before flying farther. The train tracks glistened in the moonlight. Everything seemed quiet and peaceful. He leaned his head against the trunk and closed his eyes for a moment. Suddenly, a loud "hic" made him jump. Startled, he looked around. Had something moved down there on the tracks? He saw a rabbit scamper into the bushes. Then something rustled, over by the birch trees. Tony's heart began to beat faster. Someone was over there! There was another "hic," and right afterward a figure in a long black cape emerged out of the darkness of the trees. In the moonlight, Tony recognized Aunt Dorothee!

An icy shudder ran through him. Had she smelled him? But Aunt Dorothee seemed to have other things on her mind. She walked with swaying steps and hiccuped several more times. She looked around, confused. Tony heard her scolding herself. "You stupid drunk! It's all your fault that I have to walk back!" Her words sounded strangely slurred.

Then Tony suddenly realized why she was behaving so strangely. She had been to a town hall dance again—not to dance, of course, but to wait outside. Obviously, she had picked someone who had had a lot to drink—so much, in fact, that she could no longer fly!

Tony had to laugh.

He was still smiling in his sleep when the car stopped.

"Tony!" It was his father.

Tony looked around sleepily. "Where are we?"

"In Little Ol' Molting."

Tony recognized the white house, the big barn. He recognized the light blue station wagon that stood in front of the barn. He had seen it in front of the train station in Big Ol' Molting. Did that mean that the two women with the Tyrolean hats were also guests on the farm?!

"Oh, great!" he groaned.

"What's the matter now?" his mother asked angrily.

Tony climbed stiffly out of the car. "Nothing! Everything's great!" He looked over at the barn and said, "Besides, I bet there's a vampire in there!"

"Right, of course!" said his mother, frustrated. "Vampires are all that matter."

"Of course," said Tony, rubbing his hands together in anticipation.

Acknowledgments

With all my heart I remain grateful to:

Rudolph, the little vampire, who is always on an adventurous journey when reading a book.

Tony, who has been on a trip of a lifetime since the little vampire has become his friend.

Sandy and Peter Riva of International Transactions, my best friends, who have made all the travel arrangements for the little vampire to fly to Simon & Schuster.

Valerie Garfield, the publisher, who made it possible that the American editions of *The Little Vampire* are now flying all over the world.

Kristin Gilson, editorial director, who has assured a safe and successful landing for each new book of The Little Vampire series.

ACKNOWLEDGMENTS

Ivanka Hahnenberger and Elowyn Castle, who again, let the little vampire fly with ease through the realm of the American-English language.

Laura Lyn DiSiena and Irene Vandervoort, whose vampiric cover and jacket design invites book readers to join the little vampire on another of his adventurous journeys.

Daniel Duncan, whose cover illustration shows so beautifully why the little vampire cannot travel light.

Last but not least, to Burghardt, my travel companion through thick and thin.

About the Author

ANGELA SOMMER-BODENBURG was born in Reinbek, Germany, and now lives with her husband, Burghardt, and their two Hungarian sheepdogs in New Mexico. She has published more than forty books, which have been translated into more than thirty-five languages. Her works include poetry, novels, stage plays, picture books, short stories, and the Little Vampire series. Learn more about her at AngelaSommer-Bodenburg.com.

LOOK FOR MORE
ADVENTURES WITH
THE LITTLE VAMPIRE!

Previously titled *The Vampire Moves In*

BY Angela Sommer-Bodenburg